THE MINSTREL BOY

A tale of war

By

Ralph N. Hudson

The minstrel boy to the war has gone,

with his fathers sword girthed around him.

The minstrel boy to the war has gone,

in the ranks of death you will find him.

ISBN: 978 - 0 - 9928465 - 0 - 3

1st edition:	2009	Published by	Booksurge Publishing
Revised edition	2014	Published by	Ralph N. Hudson

Cover design by
Lizz Kay
www. lizkay.co.uk

Publisher: Ralph N.Hudson

Introduction

This story is based on the experiences of several First World War soldiers merged into one character. It is their story, not mine.

Dedication

This book is dedicated to:

George Morgan, Dawson Horne, Harry Redman, Frank Burns, Harry Drake, Albert Sands, Albert Hanson, Harry Severn, George Taylor, A. V. Pearson, W.Clark, Squire Clough, Cyril Tetlow, Percy Bateman, R. N. Bell, Bill Pendray, E. V. Tempest, E. V. Gregory, Fred Smith, Charlie Taylor, Harry Wigley, Harry Holroyd and many others.

List of Chapters

THE MINSTREL BOY

A tale of war

HAMMOND SQ
HAMMOND SQUARE. HEATON.
D.BRITT

1 The Gardener

War is endemic,
and governments are the carriers.

Martha Gellhorn. BBCTV circa 1990

He'd experienced the pain before, but not quite as bad as now. His chest seemed to be gripped by a steel band whilst his left forearm was stabbed by a thousand red hot needles. He leaned on his spade, so that it took his weight, clenched his eyes tight shut and bit his bottom lip. After about a minute – which seemed like an age – the pain eased a little and, using the spade as a prop he was able to propel himself as far as his garden shed. Lowering himself onto the old kitchen chair that stood by the door he groped in his waistcoat pocket for one of his little pink pills. Taking one between his thumb and his forefinger he slipped it under his tongue, leaned back until his head rested against the side of the hut and closed his eyes. He thought of her and what she would have said. He could hear her voice quite clearly, 'You should have more sense, digging that allotment. You know what the Doctor told you.' He smiled at the thought, and pondered how her voice hardly seemed to have changed with the passing of the years. Even in her seventies, he had only to close his eyes to hear the voice of the girl he had first kissed as they walked among the dunes of the Canche Estuary, near Etaple. He remembered how hard it had been, going back into the line after meeting her. She had always been there for him. Even in those early years after the war when he often woke from those recurring nightmares, soaked in sweat and trembling with fear, she was there, gently shaking his arm and saying, 'It's only a silly dream darling'. There was that song she used to sing? "I'll walk beside you through the golden years".

It was only after she died that he realised that she sang of her love for him. How he missed her, his lover, his friend, his mentor.

Slowly he began to feel a little better. A blackbird cock had perched on the handle of his garden fork, left driven into the earth where he had been working. Every year a pair nested over in the hedge. He didn't know if it was the same pair, he just liked to think so. Now he listened to its song, so clear and beautiful. Life, he thought, is like that West End stage play, What was it called? The Mouse Trap. The plot never changes, only the cast. Life, he thought is like that, a play that is unstoppable, seamless.

The autumn sunshine bathing his eyelids felt comforting and he fell into a shallow sleep.

A thousand images and dreams flitted through his mind. First he was an infant, it was Christmas and, at the door there were children singing carols. His father held up a sprig of mistletoe, pulled his wife to him and kissed her. She squealed with delight. Their happiness infected him and he chuckled with glee.

Then he was a child, separated from his parents, lost and afraid in a seaside crowd. A tall policeman with a fair moustache and who seemed like a giant was picking him up, he felt the chrome buttons of the policeman's tunic through his child's blouse. The policeman was calling in a loud voice "Has anyone lost a Bairn? Now he was a boy of fourteen, following his father's coffin, his mother, his sisters and his aunt walked behind him. As the cortege passed his fathers friends they called out his name and smiled. Their way of expressing sympathy and their support. Then it was her, but she was a young woman, smiling and waving as she walked towards him. Now their children were running to meet him, arms outstretched, laughing with happiness. Now his daughter as a child was standing in front of him, telling him something about her pet dog. Then she was a young woman, showing him her child. Now his son, as a young man wearing that blue grey uniform was speaking to him, saying 'I'll be alright dad, don't worry ... don't worry ... don't worry.' Now he dreamed that he could hear her making breakfast in the kitchen. He called to her "Better get the kids up love, they'll be late for school" She replied "The children have grown up and left home dear"

Perhaps it was the smell of wood smoke from his neighbours garden refuse fire that reached his nostrils and, as it always did, reminded him of those burning dugouts at Gommecourt and the face of the young German he had killed that day came back before his minds eye, as it had in a thousand nightmares, eyes wide open with terror, accusing, questioning and he woke with a start, his face moist with sweat. Through all those years he'd always been able to thrust the image from his mind. Now, almost by way of an apology, he allowed the young face with the terror stricken eyes to remain in his mind. To kill a man at a distance is one thing, a tiny figure in the sights of your rifle which crumples when you squeeze the trigger, but to kill a man who stands before you. To drive an eighteen inch blade into the man's body!

He thought of all the millions of boys and young men who had died with terror in their eyes in that war and in the other wars that had followed and he thought of those pompous bigots who had stood on the town hall steps in that distant August, mouthing rhetoric about 'Little Belgium' for whom they didn't give a damn, and who had stayed behind to make their fortunes. Only once, after he retired had he gone back and stood on the edge of those fields, now rich farm land bearing a crop of wheat and looked across those thousand yards or so where all those thousands of splendid young men died. He recalled the words of Winston Churchill, written some short years after the conflict: "If only Generals had not been content to fight machine guns with the breasts of gallant men, and think that this was making war". 'Damn you. Damn you all to hell,' he shouted aloud. The neighbour, whose refuse fire had woken him, a man in his fifties with thinning hair and a beer belly, looked up from his work, his face wearing a surprised expression, assuming that the remarks were meant for him and wondering what he had done to be 'damned to hell.' He closed his eyes again and pictured those pompous, middle-aged men standing on the town hall steps in their frock coats and top hats, thumbs hooked into the waistcoats and it occurred to him that there was nothing more absurd than a Yorkshire man trying to be posh. The notion amused him and he laughed out loud. The neighbour looked up again from his work with a nervous smile, probably thinking 'the old man's gone soft in the head.'

YOUR COUNTRY NEEDS
YOU
ALFRED LEETE

2 That August

Oh! We don't want to lose you
But we think you ought to go….

Popular song 1914

He was born in the year 1898 in Milltown, an industrial town on the edge of the Yorkshire moors. He grew up in a small cottage on the outskirts of the town, one in a terrace of ten similar abodes built on a reverse slope. A short path through a small garden led from the street to the front door which opened directly into the front room. This was surfaced with stone slabs, known locally as 'flags, of approximately three feet by two feet and possibly two inches thick. Here a layer of linoleum had been laid as a means of insulation from the cold stone surface. This room his parents liked to call 'The Parlour'.

Against the wall was an open hearth on one side of which was an oven, on the other side a water boiler. Both used the heat from the fire to function. On the fire grate was a hob on which stood an iron kettle. On the inside wall hung a framed certificate which declared that his father was a full, articled member of the 'Amalgamated Society of Carpenters and Joiners.'

In front of the hearth lay a large rug of a type known as a 'Rag Rug'. This type of rug was hand made, usually by the housewife, The material used was usually strips of old shirts, dresses, jackets, towels etc. which were looped and pulled through the base material of hessian or burlap and knotted by means of a large crotchet type tool. Although a labour intensive task this produced a thick, colourful and durable rug at minimum cost. The origin of this craft was thought to be Viking, even Celt.

On the left hand side of the fireplace stood a rocking chair. Before his death this was regarded as 'his father's chair'. It was on this chair that, as a child he would sit on the knee of his father who would read to him from his penny comics, such as *'Comic Cuts'* and *'The Marvel'* the adventures of *'Tired Tim and Weary Willie'*, of *'Buffalo Bill'* and of *'Dead Eyed Dick'*. On the opposite side of the fire place stood a chair which was known as 'Mother's Knitting Chair' These pieces of furniture, like most of the bedroom and kitchen furniture, cupboards and shelving had been made and installed by his father.

Illumination was provided by the soft light of oil lamps although the way to bed was by candle light.

From this room a door led into a rear room which served as a scullery where food would be prepared and household tasks such as the weekly laundry was done. Another door in the scullery opened onto a set of stone steps. These led into a small cellar dug into the slope under the cottage. At the head of these steps was an earthen sink equipped with a cold water tap. This was called a cellar head sink and this was where the family carried out their daily ablutions, as his mother chose to call them. Always behind a closed door. The cellar was used for the cold storage of food stuffs. A door on the outside wall at the rear of the scullery led onto a rear garden in which many of the family supply of vegetables were grown. This was always referred to as 'the back door'. At the bottom of the rear garden stood two small stone buildings. One was used as coal storage, usually referred to as 'The Coal Hole', the other one housed the lavatory. Originally this had been a 'privy'. In more recent years this had been adapted by the local council into a so called 'water closet' which flushed into what had been an open sewer but now ran through earthen pipe work under a narrow lane at the back of the properties.

Hanging on a nail outside the scullery door, or 'back door' was a tin, zinc plated bath. It was in this bath, brought indoors and placed before the fire that the family took turns to bathe, hot water being supplied by means of the fire side boiler. The limitations of this source of heated water controlled the number of baths any family member could take. Usually once per week, when other members of the household were required to respect the bathers privacy and either take a walk, visit a neighbour or go to bed early. All other personal washing had to be performed at the 'Cellar Head'. Dental hygiene was achieved by dipping the bristles of a tooth brush into the soot found at the back of the fire place, then adding a little salt.

A stair case led from the living room to the sleeping quarters. These consisted of an open space which had been divided into two by a plasterboard partition, the larger of which would normally have been occupied by his parents. Now his widowed mother and, until she married his elder sister occupied this area.

He and his younger sister occupied the other space which had been divided into two by means of a curtain.

His widowed mother, in addition to feeding her children on meagre funds took in washing to keep him at school until his fifteenth birthday, hoping to give him the opportunity for a more prosperous life than her own.

Perhaps the fact that his father had died in an industrial accident two years earlier had fuelled the desire to leave home and make his own way, perhaps he'd spent too much time reading the *Boys Own Paper,* or perhaps war just seemed an adventure that was not to be missed. Was it T.S. Elliot who said 'Men go to war because they think the women are watching'? But that August the atmosphere was intoxicating. Military bands played in the parks, prominent citizens at public meetings urged all young men to rush to the aid of fair Belgium. Female eyes smiled favourably upon any male in uniform and, at sixteen he had reached the opinion that there was much to be said for the female of the species.

Meanwhile at Windsor Castle, Queen Mary is reported to have remarked to the King "What a silly reason to go to war. Over a country like Serbia!" Perhaps it is a pity that others did not possess her wisdom.

During his lunch break he slipped out of the office where he was employed as a junior clerk and made his way to the local Territorial Army Drill Hall. Here he hoped to find his elder cousin, Fred, mobilized with his Territorial Army battalion. Here soldiers rushed to and fro on seemingly mysterious missions. He finally persuaded someone to pause long enough and listen to his request that a message be taken to his cousin to the effect that 'someone from home needed to see him.' Fred finally appeared, clearly embarrassed by the fact that 'a kid was asking for him,' but he was unsympathetic, telling him 'No, he couldn't help him get into the Army' ... 'Anyway, you're too young. Hop it, or I'll tell your Mum you've been around here.'

Walking back into town, more than a little crestfallen he had to pass the 'Mechanics Institute.' Here a large poster displayed the face of Lord Kitchener whose finger seemed to point directly at him. The words *Your King and Country Need You!* leapt out of the poster. He walked through the door.

A rather boozy looking Sergeant Major, complete with bristling, spiked moustache and a chest full of campaign ribbons, greeted him. He explained that here they were recruiting for 'Kitchener's Army.' Battalions raised by City Town Halls and consisting of 'Pals' who would serve together. Hence the name 'Pals Battalions.' 'How old are you lad?' 'Sixteen Sir.' 'Then you're too young. Go outside, walk around the building, come back and tell me you're nineteen. And don't call me *'Sir,'* you call me *'Sar'nt Major.'* So that is what he did.

First stripped naked, and just a little embarrassed, he stood before a doctor who seemed more interested in a conversation with another Doctor concerning the daughter of one of his patients who had come to him, in his words 'clearly pregnant' but who could not understand how this could be. Finally, having completed his tapping, listening and prodding he put down his stethoscope and said 'You're under developed for a nineteen year old, but you'll fill out.' By mid afternoon he was a soldier, under oath to serve King and Country for three years or the duration, issued with one week's ration money – 'no uniform, these will come later,' – and told 'We haven't anywhere for you to sleep yet. In fact, the Army cannot cope with all this recruitment .So, until they can, the Town Hall will pay for your upkeep. Go home and parade at the bandstand in the park at *'8 ACK EMMA'* which, it appeared meant 8:00 AM.

Back to the office to give his employer his news. Old men shaking his hand and telling him 'if only they were twenty years younger.' Younger men telling him 'if it wasn't for the little woman at home, old boy!' Then the tram ride home, with some trepidation. His mother's first reaction to his news was an incredulous 'You've done what?' then, 'We'll see about that.' Thrusting the ration money he had offered her into her purse and throwing her shawl about her shoulders she left for the tram stop and hence the city centre at a speed that astounded him. She returned some considerable time later looking ashen faced and drawn and sank onto a kitchen chair. After a long silence she simply said, 'They told me that that you had taken the King's shilling. There was nothing they could do.' Then, with her head pillowed in her arms on the kitchen table, she sobbed and sobbed and sobbed. It was to take some twenty five years, another war and another generation before he really understood why.

Many years later his mother told how, the following morning she had sought the advice of Doctor MacWatson, the family G.P. who apparently told her that 'the Army will either cure him or kill him!' What the good Doctor thought he needed curing of, he never knew but it certainly was to come close to killing him.

8.00 AM by the bandstand in the park. Awkward, self conscious young man who joined yesterday. Slightly more confident, just a little superior young men who joined two days ago. Four men in uniform. An officer, who stood apart and gazed into the distance, wearing a peculiar smile which suggested that whatever it was that he was looking at was pleasing to him, three NCOs, a Sergeant and two Corporals. All appeared to be middle aged, all wore Campaign ribbons on their tunics. Reservists, called back to the colours. The Sergeant spoke first. 'Right, where's the lot who joined yesterday? Answer your names. Corporal Ackerman here is going to show you how to fall in 'on parade,' then you won't be wandering around in the morning looking like a lot of spare pricks at a wedding.'

After two hours of falling in on the marker, dressing by the left, dressing by the right, falling out on the command 'dismiss' came a welcome fifteen minute break. An opportunity to get to know one another. 'What's your name chum?' 'Do you smoke? Have you a fag?' At midday, another welcome break. Corned beef sandwiches and tea served from a trestle table, courtesy of the Council, consumed sitting on the manicured lawns where only recently he had run as a child with bat and ball. Young men and boys at the threshold of life, laughing together and wolfing down corned beef sandwiches. Such was his first day as a soldier.

Days ran into weeks. A Regular Army Colonel arrived together with a Captain who would act as his adjutant and a Regimental Sergeant Major, one R.S.M. Brother, complete with spiked moustache, who dropped his aitches but added them where there were none, instructing his recruits that, for example "Wiv yer rifle at the slope, the fore arm should be horizon'al to the perpendic-lar" It was said that his voice could be heard on the other side of the Pennines. But he had a heart of gold.

Ranks filled with fresh arrivals and they were divided into Companies and then into Platoons which newly commissioned 2nd Lieutenants arrived to command, young men of similar age to themselves and whose military experience was limited to the 'Officer Training Corps' at some public school. Then accommodation was found in the local skating rink, commandeered by the War Office. Boots were issued, then rifles albeit obsolescent Lee-Metfords. Sitting on the grass in the summer sunshine they listened to lectures on musketry, given by R.S.M Brothers. 'This 'ere rifle's yer best friend. Treat it like yer wife' then, with a wink, 'Naw, treat it like yer girl friend!' All this brought nervous laughter from boys who were enjoying being treated, as they thought, like men

Soon the park resounded with the crunch of studded boots and the crash of brass butt plates on gravel. Their uniforms arrived and they began to march and carry themselves like soldiers. They were becoming a 'Battalion.'

In late October the battalion passed onto the strength of the Army and orders were received to march to a purpose built hutted camp on the outskirts of a small market town, some forty miles to the north of Milltown.

On the morning of their departure they paraded in front of the town hall from where the Lord Mayor appeared, dressed in all his finery. He gave, what seemed to them to be a long winded speech in which he praised their bearing and appearance, their patriotism and wished them well in all their future ventures and that he looked forward to greeting them on their victorious return.

Then, led by the City Police Band, amid cheers from the crowds who had gathered they marched through the city and into the suburbs. As they passed the end of the street where he had not only been born but had lived all his life a small knot of neighbours had gathered to wish them farewell. Amid them he glimpsed his mother, waving sadly with her left hand whilst her right hand held a small white handkerchief with which she dabbed tears from her eyes. He thought to himself 'I am leaving home. I shall never return'.

There followed a route march which took two days and covered some forty miles. After approximately twenty miles they spent the night in a small village where the Billeting Officer and his staff had found sleeping accommodation by companies in local barns, the village hall and the village school. He found himself settling down for the night atop a piano in the village hall. On the evening of the second day they arrived at their new home; a purpose built hutted encampment on the outskirts of market town on the edge of the north Yorkshire moors.

Now life became hectic. Most days found them on the moors practicing so called schemes usually called 'platoon attack, ' platoon defence', 'platoon withdrawal ' or 'company attack', 'company defence, 'company withdrawal' and finally 'battalion attack, 'battalion defence, 'battalion withdrawal'. The attack exercises always ended with a so called 'bayonet charge' over the last two hundred yards with much shouting and cheering, and ending with sandbags laying horizontal which represented enemy soldiers who were obliging enough to remain prone whilst being stabbed to death. Years later he thought of those days and wondered how this could have been considered useful training. Surely, the age of the 'Bayonet Charge' ended when, in 1863 'Pickett's Charge' was stopped by Claude Mine's expanding bullets fired from the rifled barrels of Remington muskets. How, some fifty years later could such a charge against high velocity rounds fired from breech loading rifles and Maxim pattern machine guns even be considered as a possibility?

Other days saw route marches each one more arduous and demanding than the last one. Each march saw less and less men falling out.

In early October 1915 the battalion was issued with the current Short Lee Enfield Mark 3 rifle with its eighteen inch bayonet and ordered to the Cantle Range, near Doncaster to complete an eight week musketry course, leading to speculation that they were soon to leave on active service.

The musketry course was undertaken by all members of the battalion with great enthusiasm. On completion everyone had achieved the standard, set by the Regular Army of being able to put fifteen aimed shots per minute into a target of four square feet and at a range of three hundred yards,. Now their self pride knew no bounds. Could they not cover ground at a rate of twenty miles per day and then engage an enemy with a rate of fire that even the regular army could not better? They were more than a battalion, they were a 'Kitchener Battalion' with the atmosphere of a select club. But the training they had received whilst appropriate for earlier, colonial wars was hardly applicable to what they were to encounter.

Now they were issued with pithe helmets together with muslin 'Pugrees' which were to be wound round the pithe helmet by way of insulation from the sun and with grey flannel shirts. Now rumour ran riot.

It was shortly after this that he was granted a 'Long Week End' leave, the only opportunity to visit his home for the next two years. When, on the Friday evening he departed for home he, inadvertently left on his bed a purse containing ten shillings. The purse was still there, undisturbed when he returned on Sunday evening. They were indeed, a select group of young men.

By now he had cemented a friendship with two others who, being some five or six years his elder took a fatherly interest in him. Although they were clearly aware that he had enlisted under age, this was never mentioned. His nick name in the company was always 'Smiler' but these two always addressed him as " 'ar kid" (our kid), a Yorkshire term of endearment usually referring to a younger sibling, Always they would greet him with "Aye up 'ar kid ?" or "Is ta reet 'ar kid?" or "Where' s ta been 'ar kid?". Even when, to his surprise he was made Lance Corporal which he always believed was because he could calculate in fractions, he was always "ar kid".

The elder, and more serious of the two was Billy Boothroyd who was from a wealthy local family and who was determined to marry the daughter of his local Vicar. The other, Squire Jones saw himself as someone that the ladies could not resist and would amuse them with tales of his conquests in the local market town. Especially one six foot blonde Amazon of amorous inclination who, he called 'Big Olive' and who he claimed would bestow her favours upon him in the most hazardous locations.

Everyone in 'B' Company soon began to call the trio 'The Three Musketeers'

3 The Voyage

Goodbye-ee, Don't cry-ee
Wipe the tear, baby dear from your eye-ee;
Though it's hard to part I know but
I'm just tickled to death to go

Popular song

On December 15th. The Battalion entrained for, at least to the rank and file a secret destination. A destination which, as soon as the train began to thread its way through docklands everyone recognised as the Port of Liverpool. Soon the train drew up alongside a peacetime liner, the *'Empress of Jersey'* now converted into a 'trooper", as troop ships were then known.

In her peacetime role 'The Empress' was designed to accommodate 1500 passengers but now, in her wartime role she was to carry 6000 officers and men.

Most cabins had been removed leaving large spaces where large numbers of hammocks could be slung from hammock rails attached to the deck head. When not in use these were to be lashed up and placed in storages called hammock nettings. Tables together with benches were installed athwart ships beneath the hammocks for the purpose of serving and eating meals. Between meals enamel cups and saucers were stowed on these tables.

Troops were told that they would not be allowed on deck wearing army issue studded boots so as to protect the wooden decking. Rubber soled Gym. shoes, known then as 'plimsolls' were mandatory. Since no-one had been issued with such footwear, bare feet would have to suffice if one wished to visit the weather decks.

Once the embarkation of all 6000 troops was complete the 'Empress' slipped her moorings and with the help of two tugs left the Port of Liverpool, made her way down the Mersey, entered the Irish Sea and ,turning south put her bows into the December swell. Two Royal Navy Destroyers waited to accompany her as far as the Bay of Biscay.

So that first night he fell asleep in a hammock, which he found to be remarkably comfortable, in the warm belly of a ship listening to the throb of the engines, the constant hum of machinery, the creak and groan of the hull and, from time to time the slight shudder as, he was told the pitching of the ship brought the propellers close to the surface.

But the ventilation was inadequate for the numbers of men carried and he awoke early in the morning with a very raw throat to find bulkheads and scuttles wet with condensation and a fetid fug of stale air, the smell of which reminded him of wet straw. He sought the weather decks in the hope of filling his lungs with fresh air and in the hope that this would cure his very sore throat but in bare feet the Irish Sea weather in December soon forced him back below decks. He did not find the breakfast that awaited him particularly appetising, even by army standards but the hot tea was welcome and seemed to relieve the soreness of his throat.

As the 'Empress' entered the Bay of Biscay the sea became increasingly rough and many began to suffer from sea sickness. Although additional lavatories had been rigged in the well decks these, like the ventilation were inadequate as were the washing facilities. As a result diarrhoea became a problem. But on the fourth night at sea the large dark mass of Gibraltar loomed up on their port side and the ship slipped through the straits and into the Mediterranean leaving a dimly visibly fluorescent wake.

The following morning brought an agreeably sunny day with 'Empress' steadily following her course to the east. A smile returned to faces which, for the last four days had been somewhat glum. Over the coming day's sea sickness gradually disappeared. When detailed to be one of the 'U-Boat look-outs' he found it difficult to concentrate on his task and drag his eyes away from dolphins which, from time to time would race ahead of the ship in shoals and make a dare devil leap across the bows. Life, to him was good.

Then one day, out of the morning mist a strip of land appeared on the ship's bow. As the distance shortened clumps of palm came into view. Shouts of excitement from young men scarcely out of school. This was Port Said, a view that filled their minds with a thousand exciting images.

Then a pilot boat raced out to meet them, racing past the ship, turning through 180 degrees with great dash and lots of foam, then slowing down to stop at a gangway lowered by the ship's crew. The Pilot, a smartly dressed Egyptian wearing a reefer jacket and red Fez and carrying a brown leather brief case nimbly leapt from the launch onto the foot of the gangway, sprinted up the steps and onto the ship's deck. Here he was greeted by a ship's officer who led him away to the bridge.

Soon the ship had rounded the headland, passed the welcoming statue of Ferdinand De Lessops and was being nudged by two tugs against a Pontoon jetty onto which they were to disembark

Now the ship was surrounded by "Bum Boats" – water borne vendors –. The air was filled with shouts 'Hey! Jacko. You buy dirty book, Karma Sutra? All positions shown. Three bob", "Hey Jacko! You buy Spanish fly? Make woman want to jigajig. One bottle, three bob. Enough for many jigajig" A line would be thrown up to the ship's deck. A small wicker basket was tied half way down its length. The price agreed for the goods, normally after a lot of haggling was place in the basket and hauled back to the vendor. On receiving his payment the vendor would place the purchase in the basket which would then be hauled back to the ship's deck. More 'Up Market' vendors, presumably after paying a suitable fee to the gangway staff had now been admitted onto the ship and had spread coloured blankets onto the deck on which to display their wares. Hand tooled and colourfully decorated camel hide wallets and purses, Ladies scarves, bangles. Then there was the "GilliGilli man" who, in exchange for a shinny sixpence would make day old chicks appear out of soldiers' noses, ears or tunic pockets. The ship rang with the laughter of happy young men.

In the late afternoon they disembarked and fell in on the road opposite the 'Simon Artz Building, a Department Store or as such were then called, an Emporium', and began their march out onto the desert road to the canvas encampment that awaited them some two miles away. As they marched through the town the agreeable odours of herbs and spices carried on the afternoon air from the souks and bazaars which ran into the main thoroughfare down which they marched. Souks and bazaars which he was soon to explore and which teemed with life, with street vendors, food stalls, donkey carts, gharries drawn by scrawny looking horses picked their way through the crowds. His heart leaped with joy. This was the adventure for which he had yearned. Scenes before him which, not long ago his imagination had produced as he read his copy of *'Arabian Nights'.* But, apart from the usual vendors calls and small boys who would tell him that he could 'Jigajig my sister, ten bob', there were others who clearly did not like their uninvited guests and would greet them with 'Inglesi klefti!! (English thieves) or 'Inglesi Bastards, Qa Simnak' (an Arabic obscenity)

Arriving at their new home, first they drew bedding and were allocated tents. Then they were paraded first by the Colonel who briefed them that there would be a short acclimatization period before they moved to the eastern side of the Suez Canal to protect it from 'Johnny Turk'. Then by companies to receive warnings from Military Policemen about areas and brothels in the town that were 'out of bounds' to troops, about not roaming the town alone and not venturing down alleys, particularly after dark. These were followed by lectures from the Medical Corps about camel spiders, scorpions, vipers and sand flies. About rabid dogs, prickly heat, and hygiene in hot climate. About the likelihood of contracting venereal diseases in the local brothels, the latter advice seemed mainly ignored by many curious young men in what was to prove a short stay, for many were to loose their innocence, three were to contract gonorrhoea and one syphilis and one was murdered. One soldier was hauled up before the Padre who, performing the duty of 'Censor' had discovered, in a letter to a friend at home a passage which read 'Since we arrived here, I have tasted forbidden fruit'!

Army rations at the camp were not good, consisting of bully beef stews and biscuits aptly called hard tack. These were so hard they needed to be soaked in stew or tea to make them edible. Many said that these were left over from some campaign of long ago. Tea was plentiful but usually without sugar or milk, which was in short supply. Water for ablutions was also in short supply ,so a welcome break came on the second day when the battalion was marched to the sea shore so as to bathe in the warm waters of the Mediterranean. Since no-one had a swimming costume, the entire battalion bathed naked as the day they were born.

After a few short days the battalion was moved by train, along the western side of the Suez Canal to Kantara, then little more than a rail station plus a few simple buildings. Here there were two Chain Ferries used for transporting vehicles and passengers to the eastern bank of the canal. The day after their arrival the battalion split into four companies and moved further south on the eastern bank, his company to a location called Ballah. Here they relieved a company of Ghurkhas and found their immediate neighbours to be a unit of the Mysore Lancers, tall smartly turned out professional soldiers who impressed everyone by their bearing.

The Turkish Army had advanced from the east through the Sinai desert towards the Suez Canal but they had been driven back and were no-longer in evidence. However, there was concern that a Turkish raiding party may try to reach the canal and place a sea mine or mines in it in the hope of sinking a transiting ship and blocking the water way. Such an action would have closed the canal for some considerable time and seriously interfere with allied communications.

Their task was to send out nightly patrols some distance east of the canal into the Sinai desert, sleeping during the day near the canal bank. The purpose of all this was to intercept any Turkish formation heading for the canal with this intention,

Here he continued to live his boyhood dreams of adventure. The total silence of the desert amazed him. A silence so complete that he believed he could hear the blood circulating through his ear drums. Occasionally a Bedu camel train would be seen in the distance, making its slow majestic way across the desert wastes towards some distant destination , scenes probably not changed since biblical days,

Whilst during the day the desert, at that time of year was pleasantly warm the nights were surprisingly cold. There was no dusk; darkness came as though some giant curtain was drawn across the sun. The night sky was a huge clear bowl full of stars of unbelievable brightness. The stillness at night was even more awesome than the day. The slightest sound seemed loud enough to waken the dead. A scorpion scuttling from behind a rock sounded like a locomotive in a shunting yard. From time to time the bow mounted searchlight of a ship, transiting the canal would light up the night. The occasional group of nomadic Bedu would join them round their camp fires and share their sugarless black tea, which they drank from old cigarette tins. But his first desert dawn, seen whilst taking his turn as sentry was an impression that would stay with him for ever. At first light the eastern sky was illuminated by a glorious pink dawn. Then, as the sun rose above the horizon the desert was bathed in every hue on god's pallet. His mind raced back to when, as a small child he had sat on his grandmother's lap while she read to him from, next to her Bible her most treasured text. Her 'Rubiayet of Omar Khayyam'. Now her voice, reading the first verse came clear to him

"Awake! For morning in the bowl of night
has flung the stone that puts the stars to flight"

Years later, when he recalled that dawn it occurred to him that time was to show the last lines of the third verse would have been more appropriate for many of his friends,

"You know how little while we have to stay
And, once departed may return no more"

After some two weeks of these activities the battalion reassembled as a unit and, with the rest of the brigade advanced some miles east into Sinai to a location shown on Military maps as 'Point 80'. It was believed that the Turks were assembling a strong force somewhere to the east in preparation for a strike towards Suez.

Here, under the supervision of a group of sappers they built a beautifully modelled defence system which would have been seen as a classic example of military engineering by any student of the art.

But no Turkish Field Force arrived and, apart from a colourful interlude when the Commander in Chief (Egypt) arrived on an inspection tour accompanied by an escort of Lancers, life became boring,

The only real hardship at 'Point 80' was caused by the lack of water. In their original location, whilst the supply of drinking water was always limited, bathing was always possible, even if the waters of the canal were far from perfect as far as bathing was concerned. Here, at 'Point 80' water was brought in daily by camel train, each animal carrying two large drums. Each man was rationed to two pints of fresh water per day but most of this was commandeered by the cooks, which did not leave much for ablutions.

It was during this period that he suffered what; to him was a most embarrassing experience. He discovered a louse in the seam of his shirt. For a boy brought up in a household, although humble where cleanliness was seen to be next to godliness this was shameful beyond belief! He threw the infested shirt onto a camp fire and asked at the Quartermasters store for a replacement. A request which, in those more generous days was granted. But this was not the last he would see of body lice.

In late February orders were received that they, in fact the entire division were to be relieved by an Indian Army Division, leave the Middle East and proceed to the western front. So they withdrew to Kantara where they would entrain for Port Said and hence to France.

Kantara was no longer the sleepy place they had left but now a hive of activity with crowds of Arab labourers and a multitude of camels made a complete contrast to their last stay. The objective of these activities was to push a railway line out into the desert. Later in the war this would become the logistics life line of General Allenby's force in their campaign against the Turks.

This was the last he was to see of the Middle East for, within two days the battalion had been transported by train to Port Said and boarded a ship which would carry them across the Mediterranean. The voyage, which was to take seven days, was pleasant when compared with their earlier experience of sea travel. The ship was not overcrowded, carrying only the Battalion, the Brigade Headquarters and the Divisional band. Food was a vast improvement on their earlier voyage and, by Army standards good. Most days a concert was provided by the band. Boxing contests were organised and a large canvas bath was rigged on the foredeck and filled with sea water. Not really large enough to swim in but large enough to, at least splash around in, even enjoy some horse play. More importantly it provided that moral boosting experience of 'Feeling clean', something not too often experienced in the Army of those days.

So, after a pleasant seven days the ship steamed past the '*Chateau d'If*' reminding him of the novel by Alexandre Dumas ,"*The Count of Monte Cristo*" which, as a young boy he had read with such pleasure not so many years ago. But here his boyhood adventure, indeed his boyhood ended for, to the north the meat grinder that was the western front awaited them.

Later in the day the ship docked in Marseilles harbour where the battalion disembarked and marched to the railway terminal. There, after a two hour wait their rail transport arrived, an elderly locomotive pulling a line of enclosed trucks. On the doors of each were stencilled the words:

QUARANTE HOMMES
OÙ
HUIT CHEVAUX

The smell in the interior of these trucks left little doubt as to which of these had occupied them last. Whilst there was room for 'Quarante Homes' to sit on the wooden floor, there was not room for them to rest their heads.

On that day he and his fellows made the acquaintance of the British Army's emergency ration of that time: MacConachies. A pre cooked meal of meat and vegetables packed in a sealed round tin. A welcome change to Bully Beef even when eaten cold. But this and the contents of their water bottles was to be their only sustenance on the journey.

So began their leisurely journey up the Rhone valley, each day getting colder. Some broke the monotony by jumping down onto the side of the track and walking alongside the train as it slowly crawled up inclines. From time to time French Army Hospital trains passed them, taking wounded from Verdun to Hospitals in the south.

In Lyon a group of elegant Russian ladies, ladies probably in their mid forties and therefore somewhat old in his eyes awaited them on the platform to serve them with hot lemon tea. Everyone now showed that British trait when faced by someone who spoke in a foreign language and tried to show their thanks by way of sheepish grins and by saying 'Thank you' in English but in a loud voice. First he also tried to convey his thanks first by smiling at the ladies, frozen fingers gratefully clasping an enamel mug full of hot tea. Then, overcoming his self conscious embarrassment he said to the nearest lady , in a broad Yorkshire accent *"Merci beaucoup Madame"*. The Russian lady returned his smile and replied in perfect English "You are very welcome" then, putting a hand on his shoulder and reaching up to him she kissed his grimy cheek, adding "*Bonne chance mon beau!*". Needless to say, this incident was not missed by his two comrades Billy Boothroyd and Squire Jones who later ribbed him mercilessly, saying 'ar kid certainly has a way with women' and describing to him the advantages to be gained by being introduced to the art and techniques of love by an older woman, much of which made him blush.

Finally, after sixty frozen hours the battalion detrained at Pont-Remy, a railhead near Abbeville and began a march to billets in the village of Forceville, a distance of some ten miles. The light was failing, it was very cold and, in fact it was beginning to snow as they moved off. Marching on the pave of French roads was hard on feet more recently accustomed to marching across desert. Perhaps there was something to be said for soldering in the deserts of Sinai after all.

Two quiet days followed, waiting to be re-equipped with transport wagons, carts, horses, mules etc., the original complement having been left behind in Egypt.

Day one was marked by a copy of a memo, signed by Lord Kitchener, none less being displayed on a notice board which said that too many men in the Expeditionary Force had rendered themselves unfit for duty through negligence in contracting a venereal disease. The memo went on to say that ' the victim's parents or his wife or his relatives would, in future be notified if any man rendered himself unfit for duty through contracting a venereal disease.' Some wag added a pencilled note

'WELCOME TO FRANCE!'

Now a two week period acclimatization and of intense training began.

4 The Front Line

Through the darkness curves a spume of falling flares
That flood the field with shallow, blanching light
The huddled sentry stares...

Siegfried Sassoon

In the April of that year he was included in a group of 12 officers and 25 NCOs who were to be attached to another, Regular Army battalion and distributed amongst its platoons to gain front line experience.

In the evening they fell in on the road near this battalion's rest area in groups near the platoons to which they were to be attached, but a little apart. His group consisted of three other lance corporals and two corporals. The members of the platoons fallen in on the opposite side of the road glanced across at them but showed little interest. He was surprised at their somewhat shabby appearance compared with their own spick and span turn out. Each man's rifle had an oiled rag or a sock with the foot cut off pulled over the breech and bolt mechanism. Their pockets appeared to be stuffed full of he knew not what, their faces were lean, expressions almost barbaric but in their eyes he saw something he had never seen before. Young eyes that seemed strange and weary, mature beyond their years.

After a while a Lieutenant, who was to prove to be the platoon commander appeared. He was wearing a private's uniform with Lieutenants pips sewn onto the shoulder straps. He carried a rifle. His platoon sergeant walked across to greet him. They exchanged salutes and, after a brief conversation walked over to inspect their platoon, stopping here and there to ask a question, make some comment, even exchange a joke. This task complete, they both walked over to inspect the newcomers. Again, in the eyes of both the Sergeant and the Lieutenant he saw that expression that puzzled him. Was it apprehension, foreboding?

The Lieutenant spoke first. 'Smart turn out but inappropriate. Take the stiffeners out of your caps. Caps with stiffeners reflect the light and make you a good target. Listen to what Sergeant Pearson tells you. Then we may save you from getting shot the first time you're up the line.' Then, turning to the Sergeant, 'Make them get rid of all that shiny brass Sergeant.' Then he turned on his heel and walked away. The Sergeant saluted his retreating officer then, turning to his new comers said, 'You heard what the officer said. Wipe some dirt on all those shiny buttons and then fall in with the rest of the platoon. And be quick, you're holding us up.'

As darkness fell the battalion moved off by platoons. After, perhaps three miles, they came to a shuffling halt. Then a whispered order, 'Lead on in single file. Sergeant Pearson, follow with your two sections at fifty pace intervals. Absolute silence.'

Now they left the road and followed a track across open ground. Keeping in touch with the man in front was difficult. The man behind kept bumping into him. A flash of light, a noise like the clap of thunder followed by a receding sound similar to that made by fingers being drawn down the side of a wet glass or like a screaming banshee startled him. He inadvertently cried out in surprise. A voice speaking in a hoarse whisper hissed "shut up". The source of the noise was a six inch Howitzer battery firing from behind the walls of wrecked farm buildings on their immediate right throwing harassing fire into the enemy rear areas. This was a practice common to both sides for now was the hour when rear areas were alive with activity , when ration parties, relief troops, ammunition re-supply parties were on the move.

Now they seemed to be moving through the remains of a shattered village. Dim ghostly outlines of shattered walls, broken cottages loomed in the gloom. The ground underfoot felt firmer. Perhaps the remains of a cobbled street.

Then a voice somewhere near his feet, 'Jump down mate, give me your hand.' He jumped down into a trench and felt wooden duck boards under his feet. Then another voice urging him 'Move on, don't lose touch with the man in front.' The trench zigzagged between what appeared to be the ruins of two cottages. For what seemed an age, with many halts they followed this winding communication trench which, he was later to find out was called 'Woman Street'. So called because the decaying body of a young woman lay in a water logged shell hole near its entrance. From time to time the air some feet above their heads was rent by the supersonic zzzapp of high velocity rounds, the work of a sniper firing blind in the hope of finding a target presented by someone careless enough to be out of the trench and performing some task in the open. The night sky seemed alive with the whoosh of ascending arcs of light as both sides threw up Very Lights, bathing no—mans land in an eyrie light

At last they found themselves in the support trench, the men they were relieving filing out past them on their way out. Whispered questions," What's it been like mate?" "Oh, cushy mate". Officers exchanging notes and map references – "He's shelling trench Y at map reference 'that' and trench Z at map reference 'this'". "Watch out for a sniper firing on the junction of 'so and so' and 'so and so' trenches". "Watch out for 'Minnies' coming from 'so and so' wood" .- Similar whispered instructions amongst N.C.O.'s. A procedure to which the battalion was obviously well accustomed and which was completed without fuss. Here they spent the night repairing the parapet, filling sand bags and laying them 'head and stretcher' where the parapet was low or damaged

At about 3:00AM they were allowed to 'stand down'. He huddled under a tarpaulin with two other men and tried to sleep.

Just before dawn came the call, 'Stand to, stand to. Pass the word down, stand to.' Men crawled out of dugouts, from under tarpaulins or from under whatever shelter they had used during the night, rolled toeless socks off rifle bolts, fixed bayonets and leaned their rifles against the parapet, top right hand cartridge pouches unclipped, steel helmets were adjusted with chin straps worn at the back of the head. Then stamping their feet and swinging their arms in an effort to keep warm they awaited the arrival of the rum ration. This arrived in a Billy Can carried by the Sergeant Major who ladled the contents into waiting mouths with the aid of a soup spoon like a priest giving communion. Then, after first light came the order, 'Stand down.'

Bayonets were sheathed, toeless socks rolled back over rifle bolts and cartridge pouches clipped closed. Every sixth man was detailed as sentry to keep a periscope watch on their front, everyone else settled down to play cards or try to doze.

That night they moved into the front line to relieve the present incumbents who filed back into support.

About three hours after sunrise breakfast arrived, comprising one third of a loaf, a slice of cold bacon and half a canteen of sugared tea per man. After breakfast there was an 'Officer's; inspection of his platoon positions. This was followed by the platoon sergeant detailing off working parties.

The front line here was well dug in hard ground and divided into short bays by way of protection against enfilade fire, with fire steps for manning the parapet. It was well protected by belts of barbed wire, which were about two hundred yards thick hereabouts, along the whole front a few yards into No Mans Land. The trenches were cold, wet and smelt of poisonous gas, of explosives and of latrines. Ever present was the sickly smell of decaying human flesh coming from the corpses that lay out in No Mans Land, unburied. During the day front line duty consisted primarily in maintaining a watch by periscope for enemy activity, in carrying out necessary repairs to the trench and in weapon cleaning. The main activities, on both sides took place at night when wiring parties were sent out to repair or strengthen the barbed wire defences, with appropriate covering arrangements by more men acting as a screen further out. Patrols were despatched to investigate the enemy barbed wire defences, to gather intelligence and to be alert for enemy patrols. For those taking part in these activities feelings varied, depending on individual nerve, but to some extent these were replaced by the sheer exasperation of having to manhandle coils of barbed wire and steel corkscrew wiring stakes in darkness and over ground churned up by shell fire whilst making futile efforts not to make a sound. Not surprisingly, in total contrast to the apprehension felt whilst marching up to the front line to take over, was the sensation of the return to security once the trench was regained after the uncertainties of No Mans Land. Out there was always the possibility of being stalked, like game, by an enemy patrol or of an enemy machine gun opening up in the vicinity.

Both sides used Very lights at night, except when they had patrols or working parties out in front. As a result, with experience the amount of activity taking place in one's vicinity could be judged by the presence, or otherwise, of Very lights overhead. The Germans also used parachute flares which illuminated the ground underneath and hung in the air much longer than Very lights. The sensation of being clearly exposed whilst standing upright in No Mans land was almost overwhelming at first. However, complete immobility was found to be the best form of protection. But there was always the chance of one of these flares falling at your feet, or even on you!

It was not possible, indeed it was forbidden to remove any item of clothing while in the trenches. There were no facilities for ablutions, although in most battalions shaving was obligatory being seen as good for morale. This, by means of a tin mug full of water – normally cold. Elementary arrangements which served as latrines were usually dug out of a side of a communication trench and consisted of a sump over which was positioned a pole by way of a seat and on which one had to balance. He had encountered similar arrangements before in his army life but, under these circumstances he found the calls of nature most daunting. The thought of being literally caught with his trousers down and being struck by some flying missile or worse of being blown off the pole and into the sump by the blast from some explosion always terrified him. However, it would appear that an unwritten agreement existed between the two opposing armies. Neither side ever knowingly targeted the other side's latrines.

In such mole like conditions uniforms, even in dry weather, soon became soiled, and in wet weather, caked in mud. Therefore a missile causing the simplest injury could carry dirt into the wound and, in a time before antibiotics were available, the very real threat of gangrene. In the heavily manured soil of Belgium and Northern France this was to cause a condition hitherto unknown to the medical profession, gas gangrene.

Evacuating the wounded from the front line was another problem, the trenches often being too narrow to allow a stretcher to be manoeuvred around the corners of the bays. A wounded man would therefore be made as comfortable as possible on a stretcher in a dugout or a rough shelter cut into the side of the trench until he could be carried out 'over the top' after dark. In the meantime first aid would be administered using the field dressing sewn into the lower right flap of the tunic. These consisted of a water proof cover containing a phial of iodine which would first be poured into the wound, and a two and a half yard bandage with a gauze pad stitched at one end, with which to cover the wound. Only people who are old enough to have had a cut or graze painted with iodine will be able to imagine the effect of pouring this liquid into an open and probably deep wound. Less seriously wounded would have their wounds dressed and be told to make their own way back out of the line to a Casualty Clearing Station. These were described as 'Walking Wounded.' However, it was not unknown for apparently only slightly wounded men, making their way back to suddenly fall down dead. It is now known that these men had died of shock caused by their wounds.

These conditions also led to another landmark in his life. A landmark, which to young men who had a grown up in homes where cleanliness was achieved at an earthenware sink at a cellar head, and was regarded as next to godliness. This was the discovery that his underclothes had become infested with body lice. He was to find that to rid oneself of this infestation was not easy. Apart from a spare shirt and two pairs of spare socks, soldiers were not issued with spare underwear. When troops came out of the line to rest, exchange underwear was supplied from a common stock. Previously worn, this underwear had, supposedly been cleaned and fumigated. However, the fumigation process often proved to be ineffective and, once donned body heat would hatch out eggs left in the seams, then the itching would return. Later he wrote to his mother asking her to send him some of his civilian underwear he'd left behind. But a soldier carried everything he owned on his back and there was very little space available for extra kit.

Like all others he soon became able to identify the sound of incoming enemy projectiles and to be aware of the damage they would cause. One of the most feared was the 'MINEWAFFER' – known to British soldiers as a 'MINNIE.' These were enormous one hundred and ten pound cigar shaped mortar bombs. Standing 3 feet 6 inches tall it was the largest projectile of its kind used by the German Army. They gave a 'Pop' as they left the mortar and whilst air born made a distinctive 'whoosh, whoosh' sound as they wobbled their way across No Mans Land. Sentries would call out 'Minnie up, left,' or 'Minnie up, right' in the hope that men could escape from the section of trench towards which the projectile appeared to be heading. Because of their uncertain trajectory it was never sure where one would land. But a few yards either way was no matter, so enormous was the destruction caused. Men caught by this weapon simply disappeared. It was often necessary to parade a platoon to establish who was missing.

Another feared enemy weapon was a 'whiz bang', a high velocity missile fired on a flat trajectory by a small calibre artillery piece and which arrived with a pronounced 'Zzzup, flash, bang', usually directed at forward positions.

5.9 inch high trajectory shells were more usually used to knock out trench mortars, mine heads or machine gun posts. Rifle grenades, about the size of a British Mills bomb were another particularly nasty device which gave no warning of their approach. They simply arrived on the parapet.

Snipers in 'hides' in no-mans land would fire with great accuracy at anything that showed itself above the parapet.

Another problem encountered in trench life was the brown rats that thrived on the decaying flesh of the dead laying out in No Mans Land. They grew to the size of cats and only were moderately afraid of man. His first encounter with these was when sleeping fitfully in a dugout. He was awakened by something heavy crawling across his face and dragging after it what felt like a cold length of fairly rough string. Sitting up he struck a match. The light revealed a large rat sitting next to where his head had rested and eating a candle stump. The fairly rough piece of string was, of course the rat's tail.

It was during this period that he first, knowingly killed a man. First light on that day revealed a countryside shrouded by a grey, wet soggy mist. This condition prevailed until around mid morning when a shout from a sentry brought everyone onto the fire step. The mist had suddenly started to disperse and reveal a bright sunny morning and, some 600 yards away a German working party caught in front of their own wire and now desperately trying to reach the sanctuary of their own trench. Everyone around him immediately opened fire, including himself. Choosing his target, the words of his musketry instructor came to mind. 'Hold the sights steady on the target, breath in, hold your breath, squeeze the trigger.' The retreating man in his rifle's sights crumpled and fell. For a second he was shocked by what he had done. That wasn't the bulls eye on a cardboard target he'd just hit. It was a man, much like himself. Then, rapidly working the bolt of his rifle, he fired shots blindly at the retreating body of grey uniformed men.

Afterwards, sitting on the fire step, smoking a cigarette and cleaning and reloading his rifle he thought of a German mother, probably like his own who, at that moment would be preparing a meal for her family and thinking of her son. A son who now lay face down in a French field with a British bullet in his back.

After four days in the front line, four days in support and four in reserve they were relieved. They were met a short distance behind the line by the Battalion cooks with field cookers, brought as near as they dared. He huddled up to the side of the field cooker, enjoying its radiated heat and sipped strong hot tea that tasted of wood smoke, munched a cold thick bacon sandwich and listened to the dull, ever present rumble of artillery fire which was to form a backdrop to his life for most of the next two years. His feelings were a combination of relief and just a little self satisfaction. Had he not survived, passed his own, self set test? Perhaps it would not be so bad after all.

5

June 30th

I cannot hear their voices, but I see
Dim candles in the barn: they gulp their tea,
And soon they'll sleep like logs. Ten miles away
The battle winks and thuds in blundering strife.
And I must lead them, day by day,
To the blundering beast of war that bludgeons life.

Siegfried Sassoon

In the afternoon of Friday, June 30th they fell in by platoons on the road outside their encampment. Here they were issued with two days rations, two extra bandoliers of rifle ammunition and two mills bombs. This was in addition to a water proof sheet and cardigan, full water bottle, a pick or a shovel and a gas mask. Additional loads awaited them in dumps near the front line. Each platoon was required to carry one set of wire cutters, two mallets and six rolls of barbed wire, each of the latter to be carried on a stake between two men. The total load to be carried in the assault by each man was in excess of ninety pounds. The Brigade battle order instructed officers 'not to allow their men to run or shout during the advance' because the former would tire the men and the latter would alert the enemy.' In later years he would wonder what kind of idiot would write such words.

In the early evening the Battalion moved off in half companies and marched towards the front line. They marched with a great clatter of studded boots on pave, weapons and equipment jangling and rattling, everyone singing and whistling, full of youthful confidence. On the roadside they passed their Divisional General, standing in the back of his 'open tourer' staff car, surrounded by a group of his acolytes who glared at them, clearly regarding them as scum. 'Good luck men' he cried, 'There is not a German left in their trenches. Our guns have blown them all to hell.'

They halted at an orchard a little to the north west of Colincamps. Here they rested and ate a meal of bully beef stew. Then, at 10.00 PM they moved off again. As they passed through Colincamps even though the village was receiving sporadic shell fire, being only two kilometres behind the front line, the villagers lined the street and stood in silent salute.

Now they marched in silence, glancing in awe at the barrage falling on the German lines that thudded and flashed in the eastern sky. A short distance outside Colincamps they halted in a tree lined lane which led to the Serre Road. From here they were led in small groups by Royal Engineer guides across country tracks which led into a communication trench named 'Southern Avenue' and hence into the assembly trenches.

Now the battalion was beginning to take casualties from shell fire. Behind 'Sackville Street' near the casualty clearing station in Basin Wood a Pioneer Battalion had dug a huge common grave around which there already lay a number of blanket draped bodies, evidence of the pounding that the Brigade holding the line had been taking. This became more apparent as they entered the Communication Trenches where progress was continually held up by stretcher bearers trying to manoeuvre their loads passed the incoming troops.

By 3.00 am all companies were in their allocated positions. It was a clear, starlit night, the main activity seemed to be the drone of shells passing overhead in both directions and the 'whoosh' of green and white Very lights ascending into the night sky. He jammed the spade he carried across the trench to provide a makeshift seat. Carefully he applied his weight and, finding that it held he leaned back against the trench wall, grateful for the chance to rest his aching limbs. Looking around at his new surroundings his eyes fell on the corpse of a young soldier, probably killed by a shell burst. Thrown onto the parados, a hand hung back into the trench, fingers clawed in a final agony. The head lolled back, the jaw sagged in a stupid expression, eyes staring sightless at the night sky. In his minds eye he saw a small child looking up into the face of a young woman. 'Does everyone die Mummy?' the child asked. 'Yes, they do' she replied. 'Will I die Mummy?' the child asked. The young woman smiled. 'Yes,' she replied, 'But not for a long time.'

He closed his eyes and tried to sleep but, despite his fatigue found he could not. Like all those around him he sat alone with his thoughts of home, of his family. But a terrible fear kept haunting him. 'What if my courage fails me?' 'What if I let down my friends?'

6 July 1st

"Good morning, good morning" the General said
When we met him last week on our way to the line.
Now the soldiers he greeted are most of 'em dead...

Siegfried Sassoon

Some time in the early hours company commanders returned from a final briefing. Their news was passed among their men with the words "Zero hour is at 0730 hours, pass it on" but the message was passed along in tones that registered incredulity. Everyone had expected the assault to begin just before dawn, a usual time 'but 0730 hours?', 'In broad daylight. First light was around 0600 hours. They were being ordered to cross several hundred yards of open ground in broad daylight? This would not be the 'walk over' that the 'Brass' had promised. Now a sense of foreboding settled on those who waited. With one exception, no one spoke. Some sat and smoked, each alone with his thoughts. Probably thoughts of those at home who would, at this time be coming down for breakfast before leaving for work.

The exception was Dawson Bourne, a young man of slight build with a cherubic smiling face and thinning fair hair. Known to all as the 'Company Comedian', he now produced an absolute barrage of extremely corny jokes. Finally saying "Once I'm in those German trenches, if I can find a little German without his rifle, then, by heck, watch me chase the bugger round!" This did produce a couple of smiles, albeit weak ones. Whether Dawson hoped to bring some relief to the tense atmosphere and lift the spirits of his comrades or whether he needed a way to deal with his own nerves, no one will ever know.

Daylight came, promising a fine warm day. The Colonel passed through the trench, checking his lead companies. As his commanding officer passed him, with the impudence of youth he said to him 'Sir, you're not wearing your identity discs.' The Colonel smiled at him and replied, 'I shall not need them my boy.'

Soon the British barrage lifted onto the enemy support trenches. Almost immediately the enemy turned his attention to the British front line and assembly trenches, now packed with men and onto which he directed a retaliatory barrage of shrapnel and 'whiz bang' fire, leaving no doubt that he was fully aware of British intentions. The boundaries of the British barrage had told him where. Now he clearly knew when.

As zero hour approached the intensity of the enemy barrage increased, even blotting out the sound of British artillery fire which was still falling on enemy lines.

It was then that Dawson Bourne made one last effort and asked "Did you hear about two blokes in a pub? One asked the other "Have you ever shoed a horse?" "No" replied the other "But I once told a pig to piss off!" For a second the tension was broken and those around him whose eyes spoke of concern, nay foreboding lightened into genuine smiles, even laughter.

But the time was 7:30 AM and all along British front line the shrill sound of platoon commanders whistles sounded, signalling the order to climb out of the trenches and begin the advance. He climbed the assault ladder, almost falling off it due to the weight of kit on his back, behind his platoon commander, a young 2nd lieutenant of similar age to himself and who, contrary to the Brigade battle order but like most other battalion officers was wearing his Sam Brown and riding boots, armed only with a pistol. As he cleared the parapet he muttered a prayer taught to him by his grandmother 'O Lord save my soul this day'.

For a moment leaving the trench seemed to be a relief but, as he cleared the parapet he stepped into a world where the air was full of flying clods of earth, wiring posts, bits of wire and the whirr of steel fragments and shrapnel balls. The noise was shattering. Pressure waves from each exploding shell seemed to hit him under the rim of his helmet and deafen him. The platoon spread out into open order as they had practiced at Gazaincourt so many times and began the advance; rifles held diagonally across the chest at the 'port'. As they moved off he sensed, at his side the presence of his long dead father. On his right a ruddy complexioned man who had only recently joined the battalion crumpled up onto his knees, his complexion changing to a ghastly green. They had advanced no more than one hundred yards when they came under a heavy cross (enfilade) fire from machine guns probably firing from a strong point on Redan Ridge known as the Quadrilateral Redoubt or from south of the Serre Road. Almost every one dropped flat onto their stomachs to avoid this murderous scythe. Everyone, that is, except the Colonel. Standing calm and erect amid the crack and whine of bullets and carrying only a walking stick he called out, 'Come on boys, up you get,' then turned and began to walk at an easy gait towards his enemy. The battalion rose to their feet and followed him.

As they came out of the dead ground in which their assembly trench was dug they were additionally engaged by rapid rifle fire from their front. Casualties were heavy, particularly among the officers and including the Colonel who, it was said, was blown to pieces by a shell which exploded alongside him. To the din was now added the whip like crack of high velocity rounds and the thwack as these hit the ground around him or hit human bodies, the latter accompanied sometimes by a grunt, sometimes by a scream of pain. Glimpses to the front showed no sign of the other waves they were supposed to be following. Only ground littered with the bodies of the dead and the wounded. Those wounded who were able were trying to drag themselves into the shelter of shell holes. It was then that his pal Billy Boothroyd who, until now had advanced at his side fell, calling 'Oh God! Help me, do help me.' For a second he hesitated, turning to his friend, but Corporal Metcalf called 'Leave him, the stretcher bearers will see to him,' so he went on.

They continued to move forward until they reached the British front line trench across which the engineers had thrown foot bridges to allow each wave to cross. These caused men to bunch, a point not lost on German marksmen. To avoid these killing zones he, among others jumped down into the trench with a view to climbing out of the other side. This proved no easy task as the trench was choked with dead and wounded from the leading waves. Once clear of the parapet he moved forward again. After a short distance, probably less than fifty yards a shell splinter struck his right hand ammunition pouch, slicing it from his belt and sending him reeling off balance to trip, and then sprawl over a body. Regaining his feet and picking up his rifle he looked for his platoon but they had simply faded away. He was alone. Deciding that he could not fight the war single handed he made a dash for a nearby shell hole. Tumbling over the rim of the crater he found it to be already occupied by three others. There were two soldiers who he did not know - one was dead the other dying - and his company commander,

Captain Smith who had suffered a ghastly gaping wound in his left side and appeared to be attempting to write on his message pad. Looking up and recognising the newcomer as a member of his Company, he called out above the racket 'Are you hurt?' 'No Sir!' Tearing the page from his note pad, he ordered, 'Take this message to Battalion headquarters. You'll find them in Sackville Street.' Scrambling to the Captain's side he took the note, stuffed it into his tunic and said, 'Yes Sir, but first let me put a dressing on that wound.' 'Thank you,' Captain Smith replied, 'But no. Go now.'

Captain Smith had written:

> To: O/C15th North Yorks
> From: O/C B Company
>
> B Coy. Held up. Casualties heavy.
> Signed. Alan Smith, Captain
>
> Place: Approx 200yds in front of British front line
> Time: 8:00 AM. 1/7/16.

Divesting himself of all surplus kit, he picked up his rifle and began to scramble out of the crater. At that moment a high explosive shell exploded near the rim and immediately behind the other occupants, killing them both and hurling the Captain's fourteen stone body, together with a great deal of earth and other debris across the crater to land on top of him. Gasping for breath, squirming, wriggling and spitting soil from his mouth he finally freed himself from under the Captain's body. Clearing the crater rim he began a series of zigzag dashes towards the front line parapet. His rifle had disappeared in the shell crater but there were plenty lying around so he picked one up.

On reaching the trench he rolled over the parapet and landed on his feet in the trench bottom. Here he found himself face to face with a member of the battle police who levelled his pistol at his chest and demanded, 'Why have you returned to the trench. You do not appear to be wounded?' He lowered his rifle so that the muzzle pointed at the MP's belly, forefinger covering the trigger guard and replied, 'I'm carrying a message for battalion Head Quarters.' The MP lowered his pistol and let him pass.

After picking his way through a labyrinth of communication trenches he finally found Sackville Street and the battalion Head Quarters dugout. He handed Captain Smith's message to the battalion intelligence officer, Lieutenant Caxton who, together with the Adjutant listened gravely to his story. The Adjutant handed him a water bottle, inviting him to 'take a good swig!' – The water bottle contained neat whiskey. Then, giving him a cigarette the Adjutant told him 'Go take a breather.' Outside the dugout entrance he lit his cigarette, sank onto the floor of the trench and thought to himself, 'the battalion took two years to make. It's taken twenty minutes to destroy.'

At 10:00AM the attack was called off.

During the night seventy five men from each battalion reserve in the Brigade arrived together with rations and the stretcher bearers from a battalion of the East Yorkshire Regiment. Throughout that night he helped the stretcher bearers to bring in wounded who were lying out in the open and to identify the dead who were too numerous to bring in. The latter task was something he would never forget. As bodies were turned over to retrieve pay books from breast pockets and to retrieve the red identity discs from around their necks, the violent manner of their deaths was revealed. Here were men with only half a face, with an empty brain cavity, or chest or stomach cavity. Here were men with no limbs, even heads. The ground he walked on was carpeted with intestines, bits of men, human offal.

Here and there wounded men called out for help, some babbled in delirium whilst others breathed with that horrible snorting snore of those who are seriously hurt. Great numbers lay still, breathing shallowly. Many of these were left for dead.

There seemed to be an unwritten truce as this work continued long after daybreak, the Germans, presumably, were also carrying out their wounded. Later, men were brought in who had lain, badly wounded in shell holes for up to two days. He spent the rest of July the second and all July the third helping to carry stretcher cases from the casualty clearing station in Basin Wood to Euston Dump, the collecting point for ambulances. As he first approached Basin Wood he became aware of a noise almost inhuman. A wail as of enormous fingers on an enormous wet glass. A wail that rose and fell; interminable, unbearable. Then, suddenly he became aware if where the wail came from. All along the muddy track they lay, the wounded, brown blanket shapes, some muttering, some moaning, some singing in delirium, some quite still.

Here he found his pals Billy Boothroyd, who had lain in the open for two days, as had Squire Jones and Corporal Metcalf. He helped carry Squire Jones's stretcher to the waiting ambulance. Although he had suffered wounds in both thighs which were causing him some pain, he remained cheerful, promising how, as a wounded hero he would sweep all the girls in Milford off their feet. He was to die of gangrene in a base hospital.

Billy Boothroyd was barely conscious when he found him, lying on a stretcher outside the Casualty Clearing Station, but he recognised him. As he knelt on the ground next to the stretcher he asked him to write to his girl friend and tell her he would soon be home. Then he held out his hand and called out, 'Don't leave me.' He remained kneeling by the stretcher, holding his friend's hand until Billy Boothroyd died.

Later, he kept his promise.

Each day the centre pages of the evening paper contained long columns of casualties. This one was missing, that one was dead, this one was wounded but for her there was no news. Every foot fall on her garden path, each knock on the door filled her with dread but there was no news.

Then, one morning a post card fell though her letter box. One of those official looking things with spaces for the sender's name, rank, serial number and the date. There were several options, an asterisk and a note which read ' delete where not applicable'. The undeleted options read "I am well/ I am writing".

She sank onto a kitchen chair and read the card several times, Then, sobbing with joy she shouted at the cottage walls "Oh! Thank God. He's alive. My boy is alive!

7 The Fourth Night

Next week the bloody Roll of Honour said
"Wounded and missing"... (That's the thing to do
When lads left in shell holes dying slow,
With nothing but blank sky and wounds that ache.....)

Siegfried Sassoon

On the fourth night they were relieved by another Brigade. After struggling through trenches, flooded by recent rain, they finally emerged from the communication trench 'Southern Avenue' where the adjutant stood, watching his men file out, and fall in on the road, sorting themselves into Companies. A young 2nd Lieutenant of the Royal Engineers took charge of them. Then, led by the Adjutant, they moved off.

Behind a wrecked barn on the outskirts of the village of Colincamps they were met by the battalion cookers and fed with bacon sandwiches and tea, well laced with rum. No one spoke very much and then only when necessary, perhaps a gruff 'thanks' for the offer of a cigarette. Drawn, grey faces caught in the light of a match. Then, after thirty minutes or so they moved off again. Now fatigue began to set in and their progress was almost that of drunken men. Now and then someone would fall asleep on his feet and collapse in a heap on the road. These men would have to be dragged, even kicked back into wakefulness.

As they approached their encampment on the outskirts of Bus-les-Artois the Adjutant called for the battalion to 'March at attention,' adding, 'Lots of swank boys.' Now discipline and self pride returned. Rifles that had been slung on right shoulders where now moved onto left shoulders and carried at the slope, weary backs straightened, heads lifted. So they marched back into camp, watched by those who had been left behind, cooks, clerks, sick men, whose expression registered sadness, perhaps even surprise that there were so few. One of the cooks took his pipe out of his mouth, spat and said in a loud voice, 'They can say what they like about us KA (Kitchener's Army) battalions but we're a bloody fine lot.'

The adjutant halted them in front of the guard room tent and turned them into line. Without need to be ordered, everyone made an effort to dress into line. For a few seconds he gazed at them with sad eyes, they at him, then he gave the order, 'Battalion, Dismiss.' With the parade ground precision of a 'Guards' Battalion, they turned right. Hands struck rifle butts in unison. The Adjutant returned the salute, turned and walked away with shoulders hunched, weary eyes looking at the ground.

Now discipline dissolved, fatigue, even a feeling of total despair returned as they fell out of line and made for their tents.

Taking off his puttees, boots and tunic he collapsed into his palliasse and immediately fell asleep. Not the deep, dreamless sleep he would have hoped for but one haunted by nightmarish sounds and images. Images of a Corporal, whose jaw was missing, trying to ask him for help, of a boy, even younger than himself sobbing for his mother while trying to stuff his intestines back into his stomach. He awoke with a start, bathed in sweat. Sitting up, he groped for his tunic to find a cigarette and matches. The light from the match he struck revealed men around him who twitched and jerked in their sleep, muttered incoherent, garbled curses. After a while, he lay down again and tried to sleep. In a nearby tent a boy rose from his bedding, picked up his rifle, walked out into the night and shot himself in front of the guard room.

He awoke the next morning when a man came back into the tent with a Billy Can full of hot sweet tea saying, 'the cooks have got plenty hot water on the boil if you want to wash and shave.' They sat in silence, smoking cigarettes and drinking their tea. Then some enterprising soul disappeared through the tent flap and returned with two buckets which he had scrounged from God knows where and which the cooks had obligingly filled with hot water. Then, stripped to the waist with towels thrown over shoulders they retired to the ablution troughs where they scraped, scrubbed and washed until self respect began to return. He changed into his spare shirt and socks, even able to change into a spare pair of 'long johns' which his mother had sent him – a luxury he would not normally have been able to enjoy until an infrequent opportunity to visit the divisional baths when such things as clean underwear were handed out. Next to the cookhouse where porridge, bacon sandwiches and tea were available in plenty.

No one bothered them for the rest of the morning but, in the afternoon they were paraded, 'falling in' in small groups that represented former companies to answer a roll call.

'Jones?' 'Here Sir,'

'Brown?' – 'Here Sir,'

'Smith? – Smith? – Has anyone seen Smith?' -

'Copped a shell all to him self Sir.' – 'Are you sure?' – 'Yes Sir,' and so it went on.

Out of the eight hundred officers, NCOs and men who marched up to the line with such confidence on June 30th, in addition to two officers, the Adjutant and the Intelligence Officer, only forty nine other ranks answered the roll call.

On the third day out of the line, orders were received that the following morning the battalion was to leave the Somme area and route march to a location south west of Bethune, a distance of some fifty miles, where they were to 'refit.'

That afternoon they were paraded before the Corps Commander, one pink faced, perfectly attired Lieutenant General Blunter-Eastern who, seated on his well groomed charger and, surrounded by some of his equally well attired and mounted staff told them how "they had done splendidly!" He was puzzled as to how losing more than eighty five percent of the Battalion to advance a few yards into no-mans' land could be described as 'doing splendidly' How, he wondered would the gallant General describe doing badly?

The first day en route they marched mainly in silence. Efforts to raise a song quickly faded. Each man alone with his own thoughts, but everyone glad to be marching away from the sound of gun fire and into largely unspoilt countryside. Here and there they passed groups of peasants working their fields. Never any young men, always one or two old men aided by groups of their women folk, always shabbily dressed, faces worn with care. None looked up as they marched by. They disliked British soldiers who, they said stole their hens and turnips, foraged for eggs and were even not averse to milking their cows, nor trying to bed their women.

After covering some seventeen miles, fifty minutes marching, and ten minutes rest in each hour, they reached a hamlet where they were met by the Billeting Officer and his assistant, Sergeant Blake – a man who in later years was destined to teach his children – who had left ahead of them in Army Service Corps wagons, as had the orderly room staff and the cookers. The Cooks had prepared a welcome meal of beef stew with copious quantities of tea laced with rum.

Accommodation had been arranged in several barns and stables. The barn to which he was allocated seemed rickety and draughty. An attempt had been made to improve insulation by stuffing straw and old sacking into the gaps around window and door frames. But the floor was covered by dry and seemingly clean straw into which he and his companions sank with weary thankfulness. Soon all were in a deep sleep, the sleep that is induced by hard physical exercise and fresh air.

Next morning, after washing and shaving in cold water, stripped to the waist at the farm yard pump they ate a hearty breakfast of bacon, eggs, bread and jam with sweet tea. Then, they fell in on the road and continued their march.

Now, human beings are very resilient creatures, particularly young, physically fit human beings and the appetite for life began to return. Now they marched with a spring in their step and sang with gusto their vulgar version of popular songs. Songs which described, in explicit detail the bedroom antics of a certain 'Mademoiselle from Armentières' who, they alleged had 'Lily white tits and golden hair' and whose love life seemed to have been somewhat lacking for some fifty years, and songs which shouted defiance at the world in general and the war in particular:

'We don't give a damn about Will-ee-am
That crown prince is barmy
An' we don't give a fuck
For old Von Kluck
Nor his bleedin' army.'

This sung to the then popular tune *"The Girl I left behind me"*.

The Adjutant, riding at their head, turned in his saddle, looked back at his short marching column and smiled. 'His boys' were recovering from their ordeal.

For once the Army had got something right.

On the third day of the march in late afternoon they reached their destination, some ten miles to the south east of Bethune. Accommodation consisted of Nissen huts roofed with arched sections of corrugated iron. Both ends of the hut were sealed with a wooden bulkhead which contained a door. Ventilation was provided by a window on either side of the door, although presumably in the interests of economy sacking had been substituted for glass. Each hut accommodated fifty men plus a sergeant who enjoyed the privacy of a small cubical near one of the doors.

Here a new commanding officer awaited them, a Lieutenant Colonel Baxter. A 'no-nonsense' dour Scot who had risen from the ranks of the regular army. Replacement officers and men began to arrive, although many of the latter were conscripts who the original members of the battalion regarded with mild contempt as 'them who had to be fetched.'

Colonel Baxter soon began to put his personal grip on the battalion, initiating an intense training programme clearly aimed at forging his battalion back into an efficient fighting unit. Physical training each morning before breakfast, no one was excused. Frequent route marches of only five miles but at the double and in battle order. Officers exchanged their 'Sam Browns' and tailored tunics for the tunic of a private soldier with their 'pips' sewn onto the shoulder straps, carried a rifle and double marched at the head of their men. Musketry, bayonet fighting, trench digging. The latter exercise was normally completed with the order, 'Now reverse the trench so as to defend it from an attack coming from the opposite direction.' Lectures and training on the use of enemy weapons. How to prime and throw a German 'potato masher' grenade. To load and fire a German rifle, a German 'Maxim pattern. 7.92mm MG'08 Spandau machine gun. 'Elementary First Aid' lectures from the Medical Officer.

His name appeared on orders. He was promoted to Corporal.

8 The Whore

Apres le guerre fini,
Tous les soldats partis,
Mademoiselles avec piccanni,
Souvenir des Anglais.

Soldiers' song

Reflecting on his new rank and the increased income it provided, it occurred to him that a justifiable expenditure would be, for the first time in his life to experience the embrace of a woman before he faced death again. So, finding himself free one afternoon he walked into the local village where, he had heard were two houses that displayed notices which read 'Soldiers washing taken in.' These houses were in fact brothels. The first house, close to the centre of the village was frequented by private soldiers. The girls there charged five francs. The second house, located on the far side of the village was frequented by sergeants and senior N.C.O.s'. Here the girls charged ten francs. Deciding that such a momentous occasion was not a time to practice thrift he opted for the second house.

Having found the house, he entered and found himself in a room furnished in a manner befitting a cross between a hotel lobby and a slightly blousy bar. Several sergeants, none of whom he recognised, presumably from other units stationed in the area, sat about drinking beer and chatting amongst themselves. A couple of them glanced at him with expressions which suggested that they disapproved of a lowly Corporal invading their exclusive retreat. A rather blousy elderly Madam greeted him, telling him that he should buy a beer and take a seat. She would call him when it was his turn. The other clients now ignored him and returned to their conversations.

After a short while the Madam returned and indicated that he should follow her up a flight of stairs and down a dingy corridor. After collecting his ten francs, she opened a door and pushed him into a room. The room was furnished with a wash stand, on which stood a water jug and a wash basin with a towel draped across it, and a large bed. Sitting on the bed was a woman, probably in her thirties who was dressed in a silk dressing gown and who was smoking a cigarette. She smiled, stubbed out her cigarette and rose to greet him, slipping the dressing gown from her shoulders to reveal that she was naked except for a pair of black silk stockings held up by elastic garters and wearing high heeled shoes. Now she walked across the room with an exaggerated hip swinging gait, the tip of her tongue protruding slightly from the corner of her partly opened lips. Putting her left hand around the back of his neck she pulled his face down to hers and kissed him, slipping her tongue into his mouth while her right hand sought his crotch. For the first time in his life his senses reeled with the sweet fragrance of a girl's hair and the musky scent of a woman's body, but his embarrassed fumbling confused her. She pushed him away and looked at him with a puzzled expression, perhaps wondering 'what was the matter. Did he not find her attractive?' Then the truth dawned in her eyes. 'It is your first time?' she asked. She put both her arms around his neck, holding her cheek close to his and wept, saying, 'Poor Tomee, poor boy.'

'Don't cry,' he said, 'Don't cry,' and kissed the salty tears from the whore's eyes.

Afterwards he walked down the stairs and out of the house, ignoring the coarse remarks of those who sat around the room and who called after him, 'Good fuck kid?' 'Nice bit o' cunt kid?' accompanied by sniggers and guffaws.

Walking back along the village street he found an estaminet. Taking a seat near the door, he called to the elderly lady behind the bar in his best 'soldier French,' *'Un cognac si vous plait Madame!'* The elderly lady brought his drink and took his payment, her eyes full of motherly tenderness for this boy who would be a man. He sipped his brandy and thought about the whore, her scent still on his hands. 'What must it be like,' he thought 'to have someone like that in your bed every night?' In fact, what must it be like to be in bed every night?' He chuckled at his own humour. The old lady looked up from her bar and smiled.

The whore sat on the edge of the bed, lit a cigarette and thought about her last client. So young, so naive, still only a boy. Then she threw the cigarette into the chamber pot and began to prepare for her next client. Her husbands corpse lay rotting in front of verdun and she had two children to feed.

9 The Firing Squad

I could not look upon death,
which being known.
Men led me to him
blindfold and alone.

Kipling

He stood in what, in happier days had been the courtyard of a fairly large country property. Behind him stood the stable block divided by an arched passage that ran through its middle, giving access to the road and now secured by a large wooden door. The tack room, where he and his section had spent the night was above the arch and accessed by a ladder inside the stable. To his left stood the two storey building where the court martial had taken place. The condemned man was being held in the cellar. The other two sides of the courtyard were enclosed by high brick walls. To his front, some 25 yards away stood a plain kitchen chair around which sandbags had been piled, presumably to prevent it being kicked over by the one who was to occupy it.

Some three paces to his right, in line abreast his section of twelve riflemen stood at ease, rifle butts resting on the ground beside each right boot, right hand lightly holding the weapon between thumb and extended fingers. Their rifles had been taken away from them by the Military Police the previous night, one cartridge loaded into each breech and returned to the rightful owner that morning, safety catch on. They were told that one rifle had been loaded with a blank cartridge, although this he never believed. The rather pompous Military Police Sergeant Major now repeated the briefing he had given him on his arrival the previous evening: "'When the 'condemned' is brought from the building, you will call your men to attention. When the 'condemned' is secured in the chair the officer (pronounced ORRF FEE SAH), who will be holding a white handkerchief in his left hand will raise his arm. This will be the signal for you to order your men to 'AIM.' They will aim at the white disc that will have been pinned to the 'condemned's' tunic over his heart. When the officer drops his arm you will give the order 'FIRE.' You will then order your squad to 'UNLOAD.' Then you will march your squad onto the road, board the 'Service Corps' Lorry that awaits you and depart to your battalion. Do you understand Corporal? He replied 'Yes Sarn't Major.'

Now he waited, his heart pounding. He glanced at his twelve men. Their faces showed the same tension that he was feeling.

Shortly before 6.00 am, as dawn was breaking they began to emerge from the house, he called his men to attention. First a Lieutenant, presumably the officer in charge of the execution; then two MPs, rifles carried at the 'slope,' trying to look very 'Regimental.' Then two more MPs who were half carrying, half dragging the 'condemned,' a boy much of his own age, probably younger whose arms were tied behind his back and who was sobbing with fear. Then a Padre, followed by a Medical Officer. Then a group of staff officers, well groomed men with the look of well fed cattle, immaculately dressed, burnished Sam browns and field boots, probably from 'Division' and, presumably to act as witnesses. The boy was forced down onto the chair, his arms over its back and tied about his chest and legs with ropes. As the Padre gave the boy absolution, a hood was pulled over his head and a white paper disc pinned to his tunic, over his heart. All this done, the party stepped away from the boy and, as the officer raised his left arm, He ordered his riflemen 'AIM.' At this the boy's sobs turned into a terrible rasping noise, then he screamed like a tortured animal. A scream of pure terror. A scream that was to haunt him for the rest of his days and which was only silenced by the bark of twelve Lee Enfield rifles.

But it was not he who gave the order as the Lieutenant's arm fell. He opened his mouth, but the command froze in his throat. It was the Military Police Sergeant Major who, seeing him hesitate called loud and clear 'FIRE!'

But everyone had aimed wide of the marker. The boy was not dead and, although gravely wounded and crying with pain, was struggling to free himself. Drawing his pistol the Lieutenant walked over to the chair, placed the muzzle against the boy's temple and blew his brains out.

He ordered his section 'Unload, Slope Arms, Right Turn, Quick march, right wheel.' As they marched through the arch and onto the road, a quick glance over his shoulder revealed the MPs busy freeing the boy's body from the chair while the staff officers stood in a group, chatting as though they had just witnessed a Sunday School prize giving. He wanted to shout 'You bastards, you rotten, lousy bastards,' but he said nothing.

They were followed out onto the road by the Military Police Sergeant Major who, as they boarded the transport shouted at them "As soldiers, you lot are crap!" Stepping back from the tailboard of the truck he turned to face the Sergeant Major and replied "Yes Sarn't Major, you are right. But we are only front line troops. Not real soldiers like you!" The Sergeant Major's face turned crimson with rage at such insolence but, after a second trying to think of a retort he turned about and marched off with an exaggerated marching step.

No one spoke during the eight mile return journey back to Battalion. They sat on the bench seats which ran down the length of the lorry and stared at the wooden floor, rifles resting lightly between their knees. Some smoked. Each alone with his private thoughts, probably about the boy they had just killed.

Their Company Commander was waiting for them as they jumped down from the lorry outside the guardroom. Taking him on one side he said 'Take your men down to the cookhouse, the cooks are holding a late breakfast for you. After that, the rest of the day is your own.' Then he added 'Usually that would have been a job for a sergeant, but we're still under strength. Anyway, it gave you some experience of commanding your section.' He looked blankly at the Captain, saluted and said 'Sir.'

At the cookhouse, a generous breakfast awaited them but no-one seemed to have much appetite.

Afterwards he walked down into the village, sought the estaminet he remembered from his last visit and took a chair at a table just outside the door. At this hour he was the only customer, the late morning sunshine felt comforting. The elderly lady came to take his order and recognising him from the previous occasion, smiled. In his mixture of schoolboy and soldier French, he ordered a double brandy. Sensing his troubled mood, her smile turned to a questioning frown. Looking up into her face and feeling his eyes begin to well up with tears he said, in English "We shot a lad from another battalion. I feel terrible." She smiled sadly and reached out to touch his cheek with the palm of her hand as only an elderly mother who has reared a man child could. Then she turned and walked away, leaving his payment on the table.

Later, as he made his way back to the encampment he walked into a roadside copse, sat down with his back against a tree and fell asleep. When he awoke it was getting dark.

NOTE:

During the first world war some 346 British soldiers were executed by firing squad for cowardice or desertion, 10% of these were officers, although ten times that number were sentenced to death but had their sentences commuted. Field Marshall Haigh saw the occasional execution by firing squad as a good way to maintain discipline. Battle fatigue was recognised by the Americans long before the British.

The then Prime Minister of Australia, Mr Bill Hughes warned the Field Marshal that if he allowed the execution of one Australian soldier, then the ANZACS would be removed from his command.

*The family of a Private Ingham of the Manchester Regiment, on finding that their 17 yea*r old son had been executed for desertion had engraved on his grave stone.

SHOT AT DAWN

ONE OF THE FIRST TO ENLIST

A WORTHY SON OF HIS FATHER

10 The Colonel

House of Commons. Autumn 1915.

Sir Arthur Markham addressing the Under Secretary for War:

"Is he aware that Private G.Jones (followed by his serial number) of the 11th.Devons sailed for France on October 6th., his fourteenth birthday; will he say what steps the Secretary of State for War proposes taking, if any, to prevent boys of thirteen enlisting against their parents wishes ?.................................

...............Are we to understand it is the policy of the Government to take immature boys of fifteen and sixteen when they have set down a definitive military age ? The question has been raised time after time and we get no satisfaction from the government .... The War Office well knows that declarations made by these boys- made for patriotic reasons- are false.........

SIX DAYS LATER. "............... Will he (the Under Secretary for war) say why no steps have been taken by Lord Kitchener to see that regulations, laid down by the Government as to age limits are adhered to; whether the facts well known to the public, as to these false declarations of age are also known to the War Office; whether confidential instructions have been given by the military authorities that the regulations as to the age limit are to be ignored ?

Sir Markham: " Does my right honourable Friend seriously tell the House that the Government and the War Office do not know that boys under the prescribed age have enlisted from the time of the outbreak of war onwards? Does not the War Office know that? Does it know anything?"

In his reply Mr.Tennant, Under Secretary for War stated ".....If boys under the proper age have been enlisted it is their own fault for having made a false declaration. May I ask my honourable Friend if he will abstain from founding general charges upon individual cases?"

Sir Arthur Markham replied " Does the right honourable Gentleman speak for the Government that under the voluntary system of enlistment boys of fifteen are at present in hospitals in this country wounded, have been sent to the front and the War Office knows nothing about it? Has he taken steps to see that the patriotism of these boys has not been exploited?"

House of Commons. August 1916

The Right Honourable Mr. Watt asking the Financial Secretary to the War Office" .... Is he aware that Private Neil McMillan of the Glasgow Highlanders is only sixteen and three quarters years of age, yet has been in the trenches in France; that the birth certificate of this boy was sent in a registered letter on July 12th. to his commanding officer; that a further registered letter was sent on July 27th. and that the return of this soldier is still delayed or refused; and if so, will he see that promises made in this House regarding such lads are adhered to by his department?

In early August he found himself, along with five other soldiers of his own age group, paraded in front of the orderly room. Since his family name began with 'A,' he was the first to be marched in and found himself before Colonel Baxter and, standing behind him the Adjutant. Without looking up from his desk, Colonel Baxter asked 'How old are you Corporal?' Before he could reply, the Colonel added 'Not what you told us when you enlisted, what is your real age?' 'I'm eighteen Sir.' 'When is your birthday?' 'In December Sir.' 'Well' the Colonel continued 'We've had an instruction from the War Office that soldiers under the age of nineteen are not to be allowed into the front line. Due, it would appear, to the protests of a Member of Parliament, one Sir Arthur Markham. What would your view be Corporal ?' Before he could reply, the Adjutant interrupted. 'The order is quite clear Sir; soldiers under the age of nineteen are no longer to go into the line.' Showing some irritation, the Colonel grunted 'Oh! Very well. Dismiss Corporal, I'll send for you when I've thought of something for you to do.'

Two days later he was again summoned before the Colonel. 'Corporal' he said 'I have a job for you. There are more replacements coming to us by way of Etaple. I was not impressed by the standard of training of the last lot we received. So, I'm sending you up to Etaple to act as an instructor to them. I want you to teach them what we know they need to know. Not what those base wallahs think they need to know. I've written to the base Commander telling him what I want – I'm sure he won't like it. I've also written to the Rail Transport Officer at Etaple – he's an old friend of mine – asking him to billet you with his staff. I don't want you having to mess with those *'Dugouts.'* So, go see the Quarter Master and ask if he can fit you out with a new uniform, that one's seen better days and we want to give a good impression of the Battalion. Then go see the Transport Officer. He'll send you on your way.'

Three days later found him stepping onto the platform of Etaple station. First, he reported to the Railway Transport Officer, a pleasant Captain in his forties with an impressive display of campaign ribbons on his chest. He had received Colonel Baxter's letter and had been expecting him. He enquired after Colonel Baxter's well being and then, after some ten minutes relating how he and the Colonel had served together as Sergeants in India, he called out 'Corporal Jones!' When Corporal Jones, clearly another older regular with numerous campaign ribbons on his tunic, appeared the Captain said 'Corporal, see if you can make room for this young fellah in your billet.'

Walking together into the town Corporal Jones, who was billeted with three other Corporals in a house in the Rue Gabrielle explained 'We give the old girl' – his name for the elderly lady who owned the house – 'ten francs each week – that's well within your victualling allowance – an' she buys the nosh and cooks it. She also washes our clothes, if you ask her nicely.'

Next he walked across the railway footbridge into the camp and reported at the Camp Adjutants offices. The duty Sergeant, sitting in the outer office took his orders from him and disappeared into the Adjutant's inner sanctum. The angry tone of the voice he could hear through the Adjutant's office door told him that here he was not welcome.

Soon the Sergeant returned, his expression was not friendly. He said 'there is a draft of 50 men destined for your battalion in hut 502. There are two more drafts from your Regimental Depot due here later this and next month but the Adjutant is not pleased with your Colonel's request. He says you can have these drafts for one hour each day immediately after breakfast, that's between 0700 and 0800 hours but don't get under the feet of our staff.'

First he located Hut 502 which, needless to say he found to be empty, its occupants being drilled on the square. So, tearing a page from his note book he wrote a message to the effect that he would expect to find them here, in the hut immediately after breakfast. This he pinned to the notice board near the door. There seemed little else he could do before the morrow, so he departed.

The route into the town crossed the Boulogne/Etaple railway line and was by way of a footbridge. No-one was allowed into Etaple without a pass. As he approached the bridge, an MP Corporal barred his way, asking 'Where are you going Corporal and why is there no stiffener in your cap?' Taking his pass from his breast pocket and holding it out in front of him, he replied 'I'm going to my billet in Etaple. All front line troops remove their cap stiffeners, it makes you less of a target' adding, after a suitable pause 'Corporal.' The MP stood aside to let him pass.

Instead of returning directly to his billet, he walked to the end of rue de Gare and then turned right towards the fishing quay. There he found a small pavement café, busy but mainly with civilian clientele. He found a vacant table and sat down, waiting to be served and enjoying the late afternoon sun. Taking out his note book he began to write some notes by way of a program for the morning. It was then that he first noticed her.

11 The Girl

You were glad to-night: and now you are gone away,
Flushed in the dark, you put your dreams to bed;
But as you fall asleep I hear you say
Those tired sweet drowsy words we left unsaid

Siegfried Sassoon

She was sitting at an adjacent table engaged in a conversation with an older French lady, a woman probably in her 50's. She was very dark, with raven black hair. It occurred to him on first impression that she could be of an Eastern Mediterranean race. Greek, from the Levant or perhaps Jewish. She wore the navy blue uniform of an Army V.A.D (Voluntary Aid Detachment) Nurse, although it was tailored more towards current fashion than regulation design. The hem of her skirt, hitched up a little by her crossed knees, revealed ankle length lace up boots with fashionable heels. Her floppy wide brimmed hat with the crown pushed in, seemed to stay on the back of her head by will power alone. Shortly an elderly waiter came to take his order. He asked for a beer. At the sound of his voice she looked up. Their eyes met, she smiled.

After a while the older lady left and the girl called across to him, 'Excuse me but are you from Milford?' 'I thought so, I recognised the accent. So am I, whereabouts do you live?' He surprised himself by asking 'may I join you?' Sitting at her table they chatted and laughed about their home town, about local characters, local places. It was good to talk about normal things, not about the army, not about the War. He received envious, even resentful glances from the occasional military passer-bye, especially Officers who seemed to regard British girls as rightfully theirs.

Later, they walked along the dunes of the Conche estuary, in the direction of Le Touquet. He told her about the fighting in July, about the decimation of his battalion, about the dying of his friends. She slipped her hand into his as she walked at his side, listening intently, occasionally looking up into his face. After a while they turned back, she said she had to prepare for her night duty at the base hospital. They stopped a respectable distance from the hospital gate. He asked if he could see her again. She agreed to meet him at the same café late the following afternoon. Before they parted, she reached up on her toes and kissed his cheek, then she ran off, giving a little wave over her shoulder.

The following two days they met, drank some coffee at the quayside café and then walked hand in hand along the estuary. On their fourth meeting she brought with her a wicker basket, its contents covered with a linen napkin and declared 'Today we're going to have a picnic.'

Following their usual walk along the estuary, they found a sheltered spot among the dunes. Here she spread the napkin on the sand and anchored it with a pebble at each corner. She removed from the basket a thermos flask and two army issue enamel cups. She filled the cups with sweet tea and then produced a packet of daintily cut corned beef sandwiches. Sitting there, among the dunes, picnicking with this beautiful girl was, indeed paradise. Putting his arms around her shoulders he pulled her to him and kissed her on her lips. She placed her hand behind his neck and returned his kiss with some passion, her tongue seeking his. Slipping his hand inside her blouse he caressed her firm breast and her erect nipple. But when he reached for the hem of her skirt she gripped his wrist with a strength that surprised him saying "No, not here, not now".

So, every morning he lectured his draft on trench warfare, trench hygiene, enemy weapons and techniques, things they should ask family to send out. For example, a spare set of underwear, tins of sardines as opposed to cakes- easy to carry in a tunic pocket when going up the line. Even 'Harrison's Pomade or Keating's Powder as a means of combating body lice.

At the end of his first morning he added "Now let me give you some friendly advice. The condition of this hut, your living quarters would not be tolerated in the Battalion that you are to join!" His audience looked a bit down caste even embarrassed. There were some muttered apologies and some excuses to the effect that that breakfast started at 0545 hours, that they were paraded at 0700 hours and did not finish until 1730 hours. The next morning he noticed that his advice had been taken to heart. Some effort had been made to clean the place up.

Soon he had produced a curriculum which seemed to go well,

perhaps even appreciated, if only because he kept them out of the hands of the 'Canaries' He did not like what he saw of the permanent training staff, called 'Canaries' by all because of the yellow arm bands that they all wore. The officers, nearly all 'Dug outs' were pompous and seemed to be out of touch with the realities of the war. The N.C.O,'s, who strutted around like peacocks seemed more interested in preserving their safe jobs than training troops for what awaited them. So, as far as possible he took Colonel Baxter's advice and kept his distance.

Usually a draft passed through the base each ten days, often a couple of days between each one.

Every afternoon, the hour depending on her shift they met at the café on the quay, drank some coffee and then walked along the estuary talking of many things, never the war. When they felt they had sufficient privacy they would embrace and kiss. But finally he had to tell her, "I'll be nineteen at the end of the week. The Battalion are asking for my return. I expect to leave next Monday" She asked him, "Could you get away on Saturday evening?" He replied "Yes, the R.T. Corporal would cover for me. Why?" She replied "Do you remember Madam Rezoulet, the lady I was with when we first met? She owns a small holding on the Trepied road. She is alone with her elder daughter. Her sons are away at the war, her husband is dead. Sometimes, when I can get away, I spend a short week end there. If you wish, we could meet there Saturday afternoon and stay over. Her place is about a half mile from the turning off the Le Touquet road."

So, after the mid day meal on Saturday he left his billet crossed the bridge onto the Le Touquet side of the Conche estuary and turned left onto the Trepied road. After about a half mile he found the place. She was waiting for him at the gate. Taking his hand she led him into the house so as to introduce him to Madam and her daughter, a young woman in her late twenties. Madam, who had prepared a pot of coffee for them, took his hand between hers, reached up and kissed him on both cheeks then, turning to the girl spoke in very rapid French which made the daughter laugh and the girl blush. When he asked her for a translation she replied "Madam says that you are a very nice young man, better than those other idiots I used to see and that I should make sure that I hold on to you!"

Afterwards they took their cups of coffee and sat together on a seat in Madam's small garden. They stayed there until sunset, then they moved back into the house. Madam had prepared a meal of grilled fish with a salad from her garden together with a bottle of white wine. After they had finished their meal, she brought them a pot of coffee and a bottle of brandy. Then both she and her daughter disappeared. When they had finished the brandy, she carried the crockery to the kitchen sink and then, taking his hand she led him upstairs to their room. It was here, in a great bed with a feather mattress that they first made love, afterwards falling asleep in each others arms. Later, during the night they awoke and made love again.

In the morning they were awakened by Madam and her daughter, discretely knocking on the door. Then they entered carrying into the room a large jug of water, a basin with soap and towels and a shaving mug of hot water together with her husbands shaving brush and cut throat razor.

As he shaved he said to her "Now perhaps we ought to get married" She laughed and said "How could a girl refuse such a proposal? He replied "But I may have made you pregnant!" She laughed again and, tapping the side of her nose with her forefinger she said "I am a nurse. Darling, for one who claims to be so experienced, you are so naïve"

After a breakfast of coffee and rolls they again sat together in Madam's garden and talked about many things, about the future, about themselves. Around mid day she walked with him back to the fork in the road. There they said their goodbyes. Her parting words were "Promise me you will take care. You are so important to me" As he walked away he turned to look back. She was still there, waving her handkerchief. She called out "Please come back to me!"

12 Operation Alberich

If you want the old battalion
We know where they are.
...Hanging on the old barbed wire

Soldiers' song

In late February 1917, all along the British front between Arras and Soisson something odd appeared to be happening in the enemy line. Several columns of smoke were seen to be rising from enemy positions on the Brigade front. Other units were reporting a suspicious lack of activity in the enemy line. The enemy had begun to withdraw to new positions between Neville Vitas just south of Arras and Poisson. His objective was to straighten out the salient between these two points, a distance of some sixty miles and to fall back to a depth of some 30 miles onto previously prepared positions which he called 'Siegfried Stellung' and which would become known as the Hindenburg Line to the British. The German High Command named this withdrawal 'Operation Alberich' after a German mythological mischievous dwarf

All along the British line strong patrols were ordered out to investigate. Patrols of the 21st.Manchesters probed over half a mile into the enemy trenches and bypassed the ruins of Serre village which seemed to have been deserted by the enemy. Throughout their reconnaissance not a shot was fired by the enemy nor did they see any sign of them.

In his battalion, Company Commanders were ordered to attend a briefing at Battalion Headquarters. Two platoons from 'A; company and two platoons, including his own from 'B' company with two platoons each from 'C' and 'D; companies in support were ordered to reconnoitre a system of trenches which formed a strong point facing the Brigade front and known to them as 'the mouse trap'. The 'A' company platoons were to reconnoitre the left of the strong point; 'B' company platoons the right.' The patrols were to leave at first light the following day.

'Wake up. Wake up!' Someone was shaking him and thrusting

a tin mug of hot tea laced with rum into his hand. It was still dark. A heavy mist shrouded everything. The ground was wet and soggy. Before dawn they slipped over the parapet and crossed no-man's land, each platoon seeking and finding a gap in the enemy wire. Approaching a 'Sap', which they found to be deserted they dropped down into the trench and moving with great caution entered the enemy's seemingly empty front line. This was not like July 1st when one had to fight to control a stomach churning bowel twisting fear and leave the relative security of a trench and walk into a murderous wall of exploding shells and small arms fire. This was fear, but fear strangely tinged with a shiver of exultation. Here was the enemy's abode, those bastards who'd killed his mates. Here was the smell of the enemy, his equipment, and his rations but there was no enemy, Apart from the backdrop of constant artillery fire all was silent. Every nerve, every fibre in his body, even the skin on the back of his neck seemed to crackle with a thousand volts. The very air seemed to be electrified, his senses extended and alert like those of a hunted wild animal. The last remaining trappings of humanity fell away for this was the law of the jungle. Don't hear, listen. Don't look, see. In fact don't see, sense. He and the weapon he carried became one.

They found a series of dugouts, one of which they entered and found it showed signs of recent occupation, but no sign of the enemy. Not a shot was fired. The source of the smoke was soon established. The wooden supports of several dug-outs had been set alight, presumably assuming that the dug-outs would soon collapse. It was whilst he and another member of his section were examining the entrance to such a dug-out that some sixth sense made him turn around. He found himself face to face with a German soldier who was coming around the traverse. Without a second's hesitation, putting all his weight and strength behind the lunge he drove his eighteen inch bayonet into the man's chest. Now this was not like killing a man by shooting him at a range of some hundreds of yards, this man stood facing him. Through the rifle that he held in his hands he felt the man's innards react to the intruding blade. He saw the man's facial expression change from surprise to terror to pain as he sank onto his knees whilst trying to pull the bayonet from his chest and died at his feet. It was only then, as he put his foot on the dead German's chest and tugged hard to free his bayonet that he realised that his victim was not carrying a weapon and was actually raising his hands in surrender as the bayonet struck him.

Soon they had reconnoitred the enemy front and support lines but their enemy was making a measured withdrawal at a pace of his own choosing. He was, in fact conducting a scorched earth policy between his old and his new positions. His intention was that nothing in this area was to be left standing or usable. Many things which he thought would attract the attention of his foe were 'Booby trapped'. As they began to explore the enemy's reserve positions they were met by a savage artillery barrage which was quickly followed by a sharp counter attack. Soon they realised that they were up against some very tough rear guard troops who stubbornly resisted any attempts at deep penetration into their rear areas. First he found himself together with the men of his section, throwing some German 'Potato Masher' grenades which they had found in the support line at their previous owners, then manning a Lewis gun, the crew of which had been killed. The enemy may no longer have had use for his old line but he was not prepared to give up the tenancy without extracting a high price. Such was the ferocity of the counter attack that they soon found themselves isolated and the support platoons had to be called up to extricate them, and then cover their withdrawal back to their own positions.

Causalities were heavy, disproportionately so amongst Officers and N.C.O.'s. So, the next time they went into rest he found that he had been made up to sergeant. He was also advised that he had been recommended for the award of a Military Medal although he was never entirely sure why.

But this was a 'Rest' in name only. Each day the Battalion was required to provide working parties to 'clean up' the old Somme Battlefields from which the enemy had now vacated of his own choosing. An area where so many had met such a futile death. On the area that had been 'no-mans land' he was amazed at the litter that was strewn everywhere, particularly in front of the village of Serre where his, and other Battalions had tried to advance. Letters, postcards, personal effects, weapons and munitions of all sorts. Enough, he thought to equip a Division. Salvage parties had been detailed to collect all re-usable equipment, especially weapons and munitions. But the task allotted to his unit was the collection of the dead who lay strewn everywhere, some hung, as though crucified on the uncut enemy wire. All were covered with a carpet of black flies that, when disturbed flew up into ones face, mouth, eyes, ears. Every orifice, mouths, nostrils, wounds seethed with maggots. Eyes had been picked out by crows that flew off, squawking angrily at being disturbed from feasting on what they appeared to consider to be their property. Grinning husks of what had been idealistic, cheerful boys and young men on the threshold of life, full of buoyant optimism. Moving them to a collection point for burial was a task in which everyone had to play a common role, Officers, N.C.O,'s and Private Soldiers alike. There were no cynical jokes or callous 'soldiers' comments. Everyone worked in silence, occasionally stopping to vomit. Men wore sandbags on their hands as substitute gloves. Some even donned their gas masks.

When trying to pick up a body by the wrists and ankles, often the arms and legs detached from the torso. From the chest cavity of one body, when disturbed came a pack of fat, well fed squeaking rats. Trying to remove the 'Red identity disk' from a body, he tugged on the string by which it was attached, necklace like around the neck expecting the string to break. Instead, the string simply pulled through the neck, the head rolling off to one side like a coconut at a country fair coconut shy. He staggered back in revulsion only to stumble and fall backwards. Reaching behind himself to break his fall his hand contacted another body and broke through into the dead man's stomach. Freeing himself he rushed to a nearby water logged shell hole and tried to wash his hands, vomiting as he did so.

One of the bodies hanging on the German wire was that of Dawson Bourne.

On the return journey to the Battalion no one spoke. On arrival he dashed to the ablutions with soap and towel and scrubbed and scrubbed his hands until they were almost raw. But the stench remained in his nostrils for days afterwards.

Always, when he was alone he thought of her. Whenever he had the opportunity he wrote to her. She, on the other hand wrote to him almost every day. Mail deliveries tended to be erratic so she wrote an encircled number in the top left hand corner of each envelope so as to indicate the order in which they should be read. Always her letters were bright and cheerful. Always she wrote of their future together as though she know that they had one. But now he wrote to tell her how deeply he was affected by his most recent experience, for he had taken human life needlessly. The face of the German he had bayoneted, even as he surrendered haunted him. Surely the mark of Cain was upon him

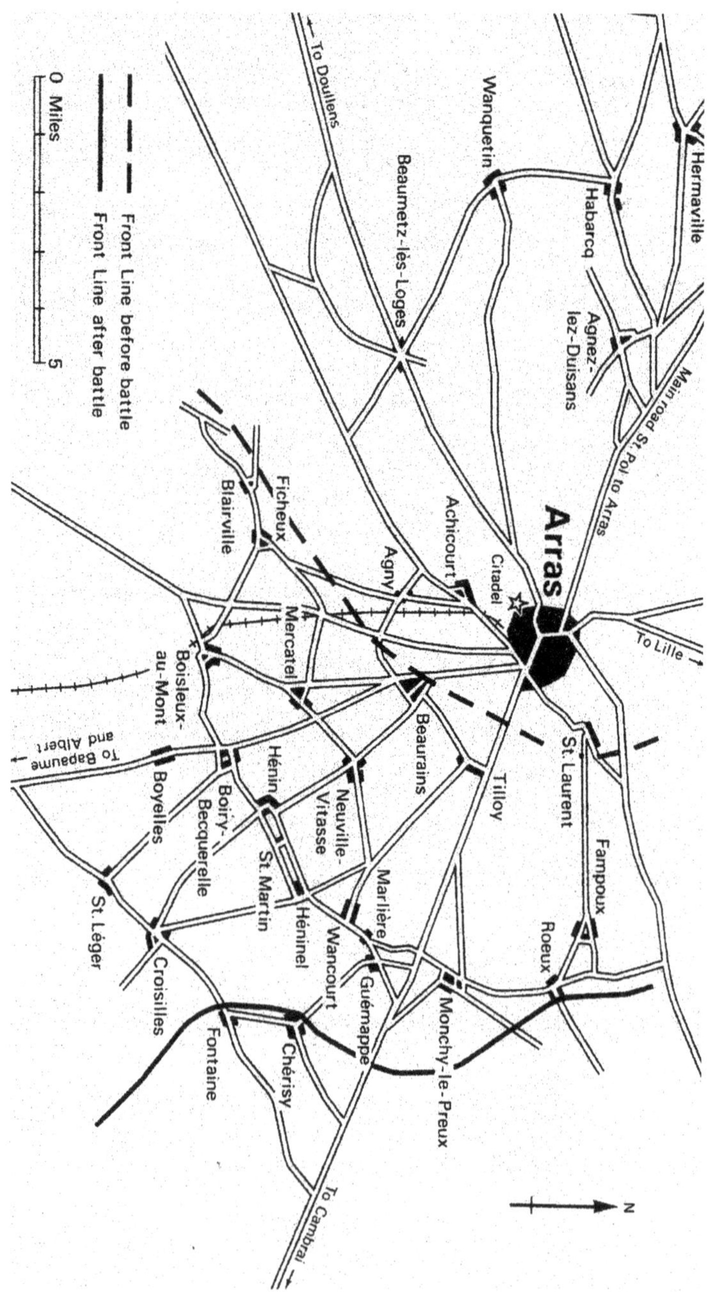

Hermaville
Habarcq
Agnez-lez-Duisans
Main road St. Pol to Arras
Wanquetin
To Doullens
Beaumetz-lès-Loges
Arras
Citadel
Achicourt
Agny
To Lille
Ficheux
Blairville
Mercatel
Boisleux-au-Mont
Beaurains
St. Laurent
Tilloy
Fampoux
Roeux
To Bapaume and Albert
Boyelles
Hénin
Boiry-Becquerelle
Neuville-Vitasse
St. Martin
Hénine!
Marlière
Wancourt
Guémappe
Monchy-le-Preux
St. Léger
Croisilles
Fontaine
Chérisy
To Cambrai
N
Front Line before battle
Front Line after battle
0 Miles 5

13 Arras

Men jostle and climb to meet the bristling fire
Lines in grey, muttering faces, masked in fear.
They leave their trenches, going over the top,
While time ticks blank and busy on their wrists,
And hope with furtive eyes and grappling fists
Flounders in the mud. O Jesus, make it stop

Siegfried Sassoon

Some weeks later he found himself summoned before Colonel Baxter who said to him "Sergeant I've recommended that you to be granted a field commission. Do you have any problems with that? ". A .bit startled by such news, all he could find to say was "No sir. Thank you sir" "Good" Colonel Baxter replied." I've already cleared it with Corps H.Q. It will take some time for all the bumpf to filter through. It will probably mean that I shall have to second you to another Battalion so that you can cut your teeth, as it were. In the meantime, as you know your platoon commander has gone into hospital with pneumonia. I have no one to replace him with, so you will have to lead your platoon in this coming stunt. Do you have any problem with that?" He replied "No sir. "Good man, then dismiss. I'll send for you when I have news." He saluted, turned about and left. Once in the open, he ran through his mind what had been said in the last few minutes. He felt somewhat dazed.

Before "Zero Hour" B Company, including his platoon formed up on the right of the first wave. . He moved his men over to the left of the company so as to line up on the tapes which would direct the attack half left, towards the supposed enemy lines.

Now he stood before his platoon awaiting zero hour. Their orders were to advance behind a creeping barrage which would continue to creep until the enemy lines were reached. It was assumed that the German trenches would have been made uninhabitable by the British barrage, although, it occurred to him that he had heard that theory before. His objective was to occupy a part of the enemy line known as 'The Windmill', a Germen strong point. Here, after clearing it of any remaining enemy he was to reverse the German line and establish the strong point from which his platoon would stave off any counter attack and await the second wave that would leap frog through his position. His platoon had been depleted to strength of thirty men including a Lewis gun team of four men carrying the gun and the ammunition for it. It seemed a bit weak for a front of two hundred yards. 'Zero hour' came with a soft dawn and, as the first wave moved off the British barrage intensified. 'What' he thought 'am I supposed to do now?' Thirty men stretched over two hundred yards, trying to keep a straight line in the gloom, carrying bayonets at the ready but not knowing what to expect. Hoping to find a deserted enemy line but probably full of quick firing Germans. 'I must keep in front so as to set a good example' he thought. ; 'Perhaps shouting encouragement. Then they might know where you are' He called out 'Don't bunch. Keep direction' But the noise was deafening. The attack seemed to be drifting over to the right so, again he shouted 'Keep direction, move over to the left'. The ground under foot was anything but good going, plenty of obstacles to trip over. Still dark, air thick with smoke and bursting shells and no view of his men except one or two to left and right, certainly no more. ' Where are the other N.C.O's, the Section Leaders? ' He thought. 'Corporal Burns, Where are you?' 'Over here Sergeant!' came a reply from his right. Now they were coming under a cross fire from two machine guns firing from the left and from the right. Then, after a few more minutes WHAM! Something struck him hard on his right side and bowled him over. No real pain and, getting to his feet found walking to be still possible. He groped around with his foot, trying to locate his rifle but without success. 'Must catch up with the platoon who, by now must be somewhere ahead. Finally, as the light improved a German trench appeared in front, so he slid over the parapet hoping to find his platoon. His wound was, by now bleeding a lot but there was not much pain. He found the trench to contain two dead Germans, slumped over a machine gun and about twelve British soldiers, most of them wounded, .some badly. All were from other platoons except one, a slightly wounded man keeping a look out, who turned and, seeing he said "Thank God Sergeant., we thought you were dead". It was Corporal Burns from his own platoon. 'What now?' Thought he. No one was strong enough to reverse the trench against a possible counter attack but, together with the help of Corporal Burns they managed to pull the two dead Germans off their gun and to lift it, together with its box of belted ammunition onto the sand bagged parados, feed the belt into the breech and to cock it. To this they added a few German 'Potato Masher' grenades which lay in the trench. Now Corporal Burns returned to his look out while he endeavoured to put a shell dressing on his wound in his side. (Three cheers for Colonel Baxter's instance on instruction with enemy weapons and the first aid training) all the time hoping that the second wave would soon arrive. It was then that a Lieutenant Dawes, another platoon leader from his company slid over the parapet and dropped into the trench. Although, thus far not wounded he had lost contact with his own platoon which should have been on their right flank. After discussing the situation it was agreed that Lieutenant Dawes would try to get back to Battalion Headquarters to report the situation and then to return with some help. Shortly after the Lieutenant left, Corporal Burns called out " Party of about twenty Jerries coming towards us Sarg," Reaching up to the machine gun with both his hands but keeping his head below the sand bags he pressed both his thumbs on the twin triggers. The ammunition belt whipped like a snake. Corporal Burns added to the fire by tossing a few 'Potato Mashers' in the direction of the enemy. Their endeavours worked, the party scattered and fell back some distance.

After a while Lieutenant Dawes returned. He had collected about eight men from various platoons, sending one man back to Battalion Head Quarters with his message. He also brought news that the attack had stalled, that there were no British troops on either side of them and therefore both their flanks were wide open. It was agreed that the Lieutenant, Corporal Burns and he would provide covering fire whilst the Lieutenants party helped the wounded withdraw to their own lines. As this was being done he loosed off the remainder of the machine gun's ammunition belt whilst Lieutenant Dawes and the Corporal lobbed as many potato mashers as possible in the general direction of the enemy. Then they also began their withdrawal. Not wishing the rightful owners of the machine gun to turn the weapon on their backs they dismantled it from its mounting and dropped it into the first water logged shell hole that they passed. Now, probably due to loss of blood, possible even shock he found it increasingly difficult to keep up with his two companions. Then, a flash of white light and a simultaneous heavy thump in the back, followed by oblivion. Now brief flashes on consciousness. First he was being carried like a sack of coal on the back of Corporal Burns. Then he was on a stretcher in the Regimental Aid Post. Someone was cutting away his clothes and swabbing his wounds with iodine, which stung like the very devil, before applying more substantial dressings. Someone else stuck a needle in his arm to give him a shot of morphine, and then marked a cross on his forehead with an indelible pencil to show that this had been done. Then another sharp prick which was probably anti-tetanus shot. Then in an ambulance which seemed to find every bump in the road, Next he was In the Causality Clearing Station, a dark tent lit be acetylene flares. A nursing sister, an orderly and anaesthetist standing by a Royal Army Medical Corps surgeon, dressed in an army issue white, albeit blood stained smock who was saying "Here's a lucky young devil. Another three inches and that would have been his spine!". Then someone was putting a chloroform mask over his face.

He awoke to hear some one crying with pain, only to realise that it was his own voice. He was in a cot which seemed to gently rock from side to side. He became aware of a "Clickety Clack, Clickety Clack noise, then he realised that he was on a train, a hospital train. The carriage smelt of iodine, Ether, suppurating wounds, torn, even burnt flesh. A Nursing Sister in crisp starched uniform was standing by his cot and saying "I can't give you any more morphine but you'll soon be at Base Hospital. But perhaps I can give you something to help you to sleep" She departed but soon returned with a glass of what appeared to be warm milk into which she poured the contents of a narrow paper packet, and , putting her hand behind his head lifted him a little so that he could drink. The powder had given the milk a slightly bitter taste. Soon he fell into a deep sleep only to be awakened as he was lifted onto a stretcher and carried off the train. Next was a somewhat bumpy ride in a motor ambulance. Then again to be off loaded at what proved to be the base hospital where a somewhat officious Medical Corps Sergeant recorded the information contained on the label now attached to his toe and asked him 'was he carrying any weapons?' He felt too tired to make what would have seemed to be a fitting response but, if he could have found the energy he would have liked to have replied .Yes, I've got a Lewis gun concealed up my arse!' Then he fell back into that velvet blackness which is deep sleep.

Next he awoke lying on clean sheets. He was naked and someone was washing his body with a sponge. It was her. She smiled and said "Hello soldier boy!" He asked her "How long have I been here?" "You arrived on the ward from last nights train, out to the world. It's now 10 O'clock." "But how did you know I'd be on it? he asked. She smiled, tapped the side of her nose with her forefinger and said "Do you think I'd allow some other nurse to give you a blanket bath?"

Each day it was she who washed him, changed the dressings on his wounds, brought his food. The Matron, a very angular woman with piecing eyes who reminded him of a bird of prey and who ruled her nurses with a rod of iron, but who simpered and fawned in the presence of her superiors but who watched them both like a hawk. "Don't waste my nurses time Sergeant " she would call to him from time to time.

Then, one day she approached his bed bearing a buff envelope with a patronising smile spread across her face "I've received this package from your Colonel. I believe that you are to be congratulated. I will also have to move you to an officer's ward". He opened the package and withdrew its contents. From between the folded sheets fell two clothe pips. The paper work confirmed his field commission with the rank of Second Lieutenant and included a sheaf of documents which required his signature. and one which began: 'George, by the grace of god to our trusty and beloved.......' (here was typed his name , apparently on a typewriter which was balanced on some one's knee as none of the letters managed to stay on the same line). The second document was called the 'Handbook of 1917' and, among other things told him that he was expected to be 'well turned out and cheerful at all times' (in a muddy trench where one could not wash for days on end!!) and to' forever think of how to kill the enemy and to help his men to do so' (in the front line one's mind was more usually concentrated on how not to be killed by the enemy!) He smiled at the thought of the idiot who had written such rubbish and who had never left his desk. It also contained a voucher to present to a tailor by way of payment for making him an officer's uniform and to supply one pair of brown boots, one cap, two khaki shirts each with two detachable collars, a khaki tie and a Sam Brown belt. Total cost not to exceed £6:00. He looked up and asked her "But can't I stay in this ward Matron? After all I'm almost well." She replied "No young man you cannot, but I'll get the nurse to whom you seem so attached to sew those pips onto your tunic".

Soon he was out of bed and able to walk in the Hospital grounds. A strong incentive to do this was that he could meet her there when she was off duty and they could be together. As he grew stronger his continual seeking some secluded spot where they could make love was always greeted by her laughter and her sayings "No, don't be so impatient. Anyway such efforts may tear your stitches" His reply "Damn my stitches" was to no avail. Finally, he was told he was to be discharged and sent on ten days sick leave. He suggested to her that he should spend his leave at Madam Rezoulet's place where they could regularly meet but her reply was a most emphatic "No", saying "You must go home and see your mother. In any case, you're supposed to recuperate, not exhaust yourself making love" When he asked "How do you know I'd be exhausted by our love making? "She replied, with a twinkle in her eye and a wry smile "I promise you would!"

But there is no force as powerful as that which, for reasons beyond his comprehension drives a young man who would be with the woman he has chosen – or, who has chosen him. This was something that he would not understand for many years to come -

First he made a social call on his old 'Billets Mate' from his first stay in Etaple, Corporal Jones in the Railway Transport Office, for whom he carried a gift of one hundred 'Woodbine' cigarettes. The Corporal, delighted that his old room mate had seen fit to visit him, especially that he was now an officer listened with a sympathetic ear to his predicament. Without a seconds hesitation the Corporal had changed by twenty four hours the date on his movement order which permitted him to board the Calais/Dover 'Leave boat'. Further the Corporal agreed to lend him his bicycle so that he could visit Madam Relouzat to request a nights lodging. Madam was beside herself with delight at the idea of being able to play a part in such a romance, particularly since he now wore a lieutenants 'pips', insisting on addressing him as 'le Lieutenant'. Corporal Jones, almost as smitten with the romance as Madam, arranging, unofficially of course, that the Railway Transport Office's motor lorry would transport his lady and he from near the Rail Transport Office to Madam's house at 2:00 Pip Emma the following afternoon and collect them the following morning 'Bright and early' before the vehicle was missed. Next he rode the Corporal's bicycle back to the Base Hospital and sought an opportunity to persuade her to join him for one night. At first she pretended to be annoyed because he had presumed she would go along with his proposal without first consulting her, but finally she agreed, making one proviso. So as not to put a strain on Madam's hospitality he was to buy some supplies that they could take with them. To enable him to do this, she wrote a short shopping list.

So, when they boarded their transport the following afternoon, chauffeured by Corporal Jones, none less, they took with them his shopping which included fish that he had purchased at the Fishing Quay, some wine and, for Madam a bunch of flowers plus a bottle of Brandy. So, once more they spent the night together in Madam Rezoulet's large double bed with it's eider down mattress. In the night she whispered to him "Oh! How do I make you love me?" He replied "But I do. You are never out of my thoughts"

The following morning, as they ate a breakfast of rolls and coffee he asked her "Does it always get better each time?" She laughed and replied "Well, so it would seem but how should I know? You're supposed to be the experienced one" Not satisfied with her reply he asked "But is it good for you. I mean am I good for you?" She looked a little puzzled and said "I don't know what you mean" Now, out of ideas about how to frame his question, he threw discretion to the wind and asked "Well, do I always make you cum?" For a moment she looked at him in complete amazement, blushing crimson with embarrassment. Then she collapsed in uncontrollable laughter. Finally, when she had gained control of her mirth she told him "I would have thought that would have been perfectly obvious!"

So, Corporal Jones collected them in his lorry, dropping her off at a discreet distance from the Base Hospital where they took their brief farewell. She wept a little, beseeching him 'Please be careful. Please come back to me" He replied "I'll do more than that. I'll come back and marry you!" She smiled and said "You're so romantic. Do I get any say in the matter?" He shook his head. She kissed him once more. Then she ran off towards the Base Hospital gate, still tabbing her eyes with her handkerchief. They then drove back into Etaple where Corporal Jones deposited him at the Railway Station

That evening with his amended movement order in his pocket plus his back pay and a rail warrant which would take him to his home in the north, he first travelled by rail to Calais where he boarded the Calais/Dover leave boat. Soon he was sitting in a first class rail compartment watching the green Kent countryside go by. Arriving at Euston station was an amazing experience. Everyone was treated like Royalty. Everywhere were Ladies with trolleys loaded with things to eat and drink. People smiled, cheered, and patted them on the back. He felt so sorry for the Tommie's who were clearly embarrassed by their filthy, mud stained state, all the civilians seemed so clean. One Tommy asked him, as though seeking advice "How can I go home to my Mum like this Sir? I'm lousy" He could think of nothing to say to the lad except "I'm sure she won't care as long as she has you home"

He changed his money into sterling and made his way, first by the underground to Kings Cross and then onto a train for the north. He thought of sending his mother a telegram to tell her of his news but, thinking of the effect of a Telegram Boy arriving on the doorstep would have had on her he decided to arrive unexpected.

Some weary hours later he arrived at the L.N.E.R.station and walked through the town to the tram stop where he joined a line of waiting people. He was the cause of some curiosity, this soldier who wore a private soldier's uniform with 2nd.Lieutenants insignia sewn onto the shoulder straps of his tunic and who carried a kitbag. He ignored the attention and, when the tram arrived ran up the stairs onto the upper deck where he lit a cigarette. He offered the ticket collector the penny fare but the man refused to take it. Finally, he stepped off the tram, shouldered his kit bag and walked up the street to his home. Walking down the short front garden path he opened the door and called out "Mum, I'm home!"

On hearing his voice his mother ran out of the kitchen scullery, hands covered in baking powder, followed by his elder sister and threw her arms around him sobbing "Oh love, you should have told me you were coming!"

So began his ten days leave. The first evening a continual column of people came through the door. Initially neighbours then, as news of his arrival spread, relatives. Women crying, men pumping his hand, little boys asking a thousand questions as only little boys can. That night he sank between warm flannelette sheets in his own bed and fell into a dreamless sleep. The following morning he arose late, washed and shaved at the cellar head sink and dressed himself in his civilian clothes. After eating a breakfast of bacon, fried eggs and fried bread without a thought about food scarcity he sat on the opposite side of the fireplace and talked with his mother about many things. He told her about the girl, showing her a photograph he carried. He also told her that he thought that the girl was Jewish, that her parents lived in the better part of town and that he planned to visit them. She listened silently to all this, finally saying "If you love each other, that is all that matters. However, keep all this from your relatives for the time being. You know what they're like about religion"

Nonetheless, his mother did haul him off to Chapel on the following Sunday morning. The chance to 'show him off' was too important to miss.

So the following morning, putting the voucher in his pocket he set out for town to place an order for his uniform, but first he took the tram from the town centre out to where the girls' parents lived. He found them warm and friendly. They had received a letter from their daughter to say that they could expect his visit. They did not ask of his religion, neither did he volunteer any information.

When he tried to take his leave, saying he must find a tailor, her father exclaimed, "But I am a tailor. I insist that you allow me to be your tailor". So now her father travelled back into town with him and took him to his shop in the very up market 'Victoria and Albert Arcade' where two other tailors each sat cross legged before two large windows, busily stitching suits of one sort or another. Then followed, for him a unique experience of being "measured". A pleasant and friendly experience, being asked many questions about the war and many questions about clothes that he had never been asked before. Some of his answers brought forth gales of laughter, for example when they had to explain what was meant by the question "On which side do you dress." And, of course many questions about his daughter. How was she, did she get enough sleep, when did he last see her etc.? Questions any father would ask a young man who his daughter appeared to have chosen. But this was something that life had yet to teach him. Finally, after being asked to go back for a fitting in two days time he took his leave and made for home, deciding to walk back through the park. Walking alone, thinking about his visit to her parents home, it occurred to him that they were largely 'classless' in their outlook on life.

It was here that a young lady stopped in front of him and presented him with a white feather which, much to the girl's surprise, made him almost collapse with laughter. The young lady clearly thought he was raving mad and beat a hasty retreat.

Ten days flew by and he found himself at Euston station, wearing an officer's uniform the quality of which far exceeded the value of the government voucher and with a movement order in his pocket which instructed him to report to the 9th.Battalion, presently situated near St. Omer. The scene was a sad, nay terrible sight, The platform was packed with wives, children, sweethearts saying good by – many literally for the last time- to their loved ones Elderly, watery eyed men, biting their lower lip in an effort to fight back tears whilst trying to smile, saying good by to their sons.

He boarded the train and took a seat in a crowded First Class compartment. He felt a great relief when the train began to pull out of the station. All was quiet; no one spoke, each avoiding eye contact. Once well clear of London, the silence was broken. People began to chat. Someone asked "Why are we fighting this war?" Another suggested that it was for the benefit of those who were making millions from the manufacture of munitions. No one, it appeared had a counter argument.

On arrival in Calais he sought the Railway Transport Officer who informed him that the 9th Battalion were to be found some twelve miles away, that motor transport had been arranged for him and for six other ranks who were returning from leave and who were hanging around the Rail Transport Officer's office door looking glum and forgotten. Soon a British Army 'open bed' lorry arrived. He threw his kit bag into the back, along with the kit of the others and climbed in beside the driver.

On arriving at Battalion he was dropped off at the Officers' mess where he asked for the Adjutant. After a few moments an elderly, tired looking Major appeared hand outstretched and smiling, saying "Welcome my boy, welcome. We've been expecting you. The R.T.O. in Calais 'phoned to say that you were on your way. Everyone, including the Colonel is waiting to meet you. Come, have a drink with us." With this he led him into a makeshift bar, grouped around which were the Battalion officers, including the Colonel who thrust a glass of whiskey into his hand and called "Let us all drink a toast of welcome to our new brother officer" Everyone responded with "To our new brother officer!" and tossed the contents of their glass down their throats. Now people pushed forward to introduce themselves. By the tone of their voices he got a distinct impression that his "Welcome" party had started some while ago. Next, the Colonel introduced him to his Company Commander, a Captain Procter who, although still sober, clearly wasn't feeling too much pain either and who assured him that his platoon was a "perfectly splendid bunch of chaps. Includes some new blokes though".

Soon, a party developed the likes of which he had never experienced before. First the Adjutant recited his party piece in what was supposed to be a cockney accent.

'There's a gentleman's urinal to the norf of Waterloo,
There's an'uver one for women fur'ver da'an.
There's a girl there, Alice Billing. You can have her for a shilling
An' she'll stay with you all night for half a craawn.'

Not to be out done, the Colonel now countered with his party piece.

'Uncle Joe and Auntie Mabel
Fainted at the breakfast table.
Wasn't that sufficient warning not to do it in the morning?
But Ovaltine has put them right;
Now they do it every night.
Uncle Joe is hoping soon
To do it in the afternoon!'

His attempt to pay for a round was rejected with 'Wouldn't hear of it old boy' He did, however persuade the company that perhaps, since he was returning from 'sick leave' that he should stick to beer. The Medical Officer then asked for silence -"This" the Colonel whispered, "Is the M.O.'s party piece" -

Calling

"Gentlemen, I give you a toast:

'Here's to the girl who lives on the hill.

She say's she won't but her sister will"

Everyone raised their glass and dutifully replied

"The Girl who lives on the hill!"

Now the Padre lifted his glass and sang

"My eldest sister Lily

Is a whore in Piccadilly"

Where upon everyone joined in

"And my Mother is another on the Strand

And my brother hawks his arsehole

Round the Elephant an' Castle

We're the finest bleedin' family in the land!"

Finally he asked the Colonel if he may be excused. He left a mess party which seemed to think that there was no to-morrow. As he left the mess a young soldier stepped up to him, saluted smartly and said "Excuse me sir, my name is Jones. I'm your batman. I've got your valise (diplomatically referring to his Private Soldiers kit bag). Would you like me to show you to your sleeping quarters?" This was something new which had not crossed his mind. Later, he sat on his cot in a tent he was to share with one other 2nd.Lieutenant and considered what he had experienced over the last couple of hours. His first experience as a member of an officer's mess. "So much" he thought "for the prejudice he had thought an ex ranker officer could expect to encounter" That may have been the case in 1914, but did not appear to apply in a battle hardened Battalion.

The following morning Captain Procter introduced him to his platoon sergeant, a regular soldier named William Morgan who had the platoon 'paraded' for his inspection. He told him that the platoon were ' not a bad lot' but more than a few were conscripts, drafted in as casualty replacements and who were 'a bit green' and resentful at being in the Army.

As they approached the platoon Sergeant Morgan called them to attention. He asked the Sergeant to 'stand them at ease' Then he addressed them by saying "So I don't have to address everyone as 'Hey, you' you can all tell me your name and something about yourself. For example, how long you've been with the Battalion, how long you've been in the Army, where you're from etc." So, he and Sergeant Morgan walked down the two ranks, stopping at each soldier. Each man came to attention and, in answer to his questions said "Private so & so Sir. Been with the Battalion since '15 Sir" and so on. As they reached the end of the rear rank he heard a whispered snide remark "They've sent a kid to boss us, an ex ranker at that!" The Sergeant pretended not to have heard, although there was little doubt that he had. So, he turned to him and said in a loud clear voice "Alright Sergeant, lets see if we can work up their appetites. Dismiss the platoon. Fall in again here, in 'Battle Order' in ten minutes" With that he turned on his heel and walked swiftly back to his quarter,

Fifteen minutes later he returned, dressed in his privates' uniform with pips sewn on the shoulder straps. As he approached, Sergeant Morgan called them to attention. He said, "Thank you Sergeant" then ordered "Platoon sloop arms, right turn, trail arms, DOUBLE MARCH.

They doubled through the camp, past a startled sentry outside the Guard Room, returning his smart 'Present Arms" with "Eye's right!' 'Eyes Front!', Then, as they ran onto the road, 'Left wheel'. When they had covered what he estimated to be about two miles he gave the order 'About turn'. Then, a right wheel back into the camp, past the Guard Room, returning the somewhat perplexed sentry's "Present" with "Eyes Left! Eyes Front " and came to a halt at their starting point.

Turning them into line he said 'That was about four miles. We'll fall in tomorrow at 5:30 Ack Emma, in 'Battle Order' but this time we'll do five miles. For the benefit of those of you who have not yet been in the line! Your comrades will tell you that, apart from Jerry trying to bump you off, you need to be fit to survive. We are going to be the fittest platoon in the Battalion. Then, tomorrow afternoon there will be a kit inspection. In addition to clean rifles I shall expect to see clean kit. So if you've stuffed a 'cootie' (meaning lice infested) shirt and a pair of sweaty socks into your kit bag hoping that they would cool off, I would strongly advise you this afternoon to visit one of the houses in the village who offer to do soldiers washing – and I don't mean the brothel – this remark brought forth some laughter-. Thank you Sergeant. You may dismiss the platoon" Sergeant Morgan saluted him, a sly smile touching the corners of his mouth.

That evening, after taking his evening meal in the mess, Captain Procter approached him. "I heard a story about you and your platoon dashing down the road at the double this afternoon. What was that about?" He replied "I detected an element that would show me 'who was boss'. I thought I ought to put the record straight sir. . Captain Procter smiled and said "They picked the wrong chap, didn't they?" He replied "Yes sir, I think perhaps they did" adding "We'll be doing the same again before breakfast tomorrow. Followed by the threat of a kit inspection. That is, unless you have other plans for them."

The fact that they arrived for breakfast having done a run of some miles in 'Battle Order' and, although sweating by no means winded became a matter of pride. Something which set them apart from other platoons. The fact that they had a platoon commander who ran at their head, like them in Battle Order and carrying a rifle only added to their sense of pride. Soon they became a closely knit unit.

14 Passchendael

I died in Hell, (They called it
Passchendael)
My wound was slight
And I was hobbling back; then a shell
Burst slick upon the duck-boards; so I fell
Into the bottomless mud, and lost the light

Siegfried Sassoon

The Battalion he had joined at St Omer, indeed the Division were now each day practicing an attack. Troops attacked enemy positions and Pill Boxes represented by tapes whilst Staff Officers galloped around with great dash and splendour and later discussed the day's events with great enthusiasm and detail.

The last rest before the battle was in Mill camp near the village of Watou where the Battalion arrived in the afternoon of October 3rd,

On October 5th a period of three hours compulsory silence was ordered throughout the Battalion. Men read, wrote letters or simply went to sleep. At 7:30pm, the Battalion marched two miles to the 'embussing Point' from where they were taken by commandeered London double Decker buses to Vlamartinghe. The night was very dark and quiet with some rain when they arrived. Here they began a march in single file through Ypres on the St.Jean/Wieltje Road and then some six kilometres over recently conquered ground to Spree Farm, one and a half miles north east of Wieltje , arriving at dawn.

It was a cold miserable dawn, the only landmarks in the grey wastes were a few 'Pill boxes, several derelict tanks, stumps of trees and a duckboard causeway, created by Labour Battalions and known as '6 track', winding towards a location near where it crossed the Langemark/ Zonnebeke Road and known as 'Kansas Cross' The billets were shell holes in Flanders mud. The whole area was crowded with troops and littered with the debris of battle. The ground, over two years had been churned up by thousands, if not hundreds of thousands of shells that had destroyed an ancient drainage system which now, with the addition of incessant rain had turned the land back into the morass that it originally was. Labour battalions were busy building a straight plank road across the mud and what seemed to be thousands of men were building tracks which led to gun positions and dumps on either side of this plank road, the only practical method of communication on a front of some two miles. Hundreds of mules carrying ammunition and supplies struggled forward on either side of the plank road. Transport Wagons and motor Lorries went as far forward as possible but every thirty minutes or so one would slip off the track and into the mud, causing an obstruction. Transport Wagons were lifted back onto the planks but with a loaded motor transport this could not be done so the motor vehicle would be tipped off into the mud and the long endless line of traffic moved on again. On either side of the track was littered with the flotsam of war. Dozens of derelict motor vehicles, thousands of shells, hundreds of dead horses and mules all rapidly sinking into the mud. The enemy constantly shelled the plank road and every 'Hit', and there were many caused casualties. But the plank road was quickly repaired and the endless column moved on. A good landmark, near Kansas Cross was a burnt out motor lorry which, loaded with petrol cans had been hit by a shell and set ablaze, killing the driver whose incinerated body still sat slumped over the steering wheel. This landmark was known as 'The incinerated Man'.

The Battalion spent the next day at a location known as 'Spree Farm' making final preparations for the coming battle. Enemy shelling was sporadic although several men were killed when a shell scored a hit on a dugout near Battalion Headquarters. The rain was incessant and by mid morning he, like everyone else was soaked through and were to remain so for the days to come. The next morning was dry and sunny which, after two days spent in a shell hole he found welcome but, In the afternoon the rain returned and was continuous and without pause for twelve hours.

It was only 2,500 yards to the assembly point for the attack. As it was important not to arrive too early the Battalion moved off at 2:30AM – three hours before Zero Hour – but instead of taking the estimated 45 minutes to cover the distance it took three hours and it was almost zero hour when they finally arrived at their assembly point. But the worst part of the journey was the last thousand yards which took two hours. Later, one of the Battalion scouts told him how they had found a man from the another Territorial Battalion who had been stuck in a shell hole for some hours and was near to complete exhaustion, his struggles only embedded him further into the mud. Taking two volunteers, they followed the scout back to this poor fellow. After struggling for some minutes they managed to free the man and wanted to take him to a place of safety. But the man would have none of it. .Although extremely exhausted, all he would say was "I must have my rifle" – which was have half buried in mud and, therefore useless-. "I must go over with 'B' Company"

They flopped down into ancient muddy trenches, hoping for a brief respite before the attack began. Company Commanders served a generous tot of rum to all. As a grey, watery dawn appeared they lined the tapes and, as the barrage opened up, moved off in a rough extended order toward the crest of Passchendael Ridge. The man on his immediate left took a bullet in his head, gave a grunt and fell face first into the mud, a hole in the back of his skull the size of a saucer. But the plan, which called for them to closely follow a creeping barrage was impossible to achieve as they tried to progress through cloying oozing grey Flanders mud so that, when the barrage lifted over "Pill Box Avenue" they were still slipping, floundering through calf deep mud. A determined and alert enemy now poured into them accurate rifle and machine gun fire and called down artillery fire onto their ranks. Fortunately the shells sank deep into the mud before exploding which minimized their destructive power.

The attack stalled, casualties were heavy. It was not possible to go forward nor, due to machine guns firing in enfilade on both their flanks plus the enemy barrage which was landing behind them was it possible to withdraw. All that could be done was to form a rough, hopefully defensive line of suitable situated shell holes. The morning passed into afternoon and neither artillery nor small arms fire showed any signs of abating. Men were stuck in mud all over the battlefield, imploring help to lift them out; half crazy with the sense of their own impotence under such enemy fire, but it was impossible to reach them. The battle field was littered with wounded who, having fallen into shell holes unconscious or unable to move simply sank into the mud and drowned. So began the most miserable three days and two nights in all his war, his platoon reduced to some twenty men pinned down in four shell craters with no food or water other than their iron rations and the contents of their water bottles. It was impossible to move in daylight, to show oneself above the rim of the crater was to invite a head shot from accurate and determined snipers.

After darkness fell he crawled out into the open to rob the dead of their rations, water bottles and ammunition which he distributed among his men.

With the help of two members of his platoon, he managed to get three wounded into shelter and to dress their wounds. He sent a man down to the dressing station near a pill box named Calgary Grange with instructions to return with some stretcher bearers so as to evacuate his wounded, which he did. Calgary Grange was a medium size pill box capable of holding about ten men with two bunks on either side. Floor to ceiling it was about five feet high and about five steps down from the entrance to the floor. The stretcher bearers told him that there were probably about ninety stretcher cases lying around the pill box, most of whom had been waiting for attention for twenty four hours and that the Battalion medical officers were working like men possessed.

It is said that necessity is the mother of invention and, each day after dark they brewed themselves a billycan of tea on a tiny "Tommy Cooker" crouching over it to shield the light with their bodies. Each night he crawled to check each of the posts manned by his depleted platoon. On the third night, soon after dark he heard a voice with an antipodean's accent asking "where's your company headquarters mate?" It was the Kiwis, the 3rd.Brigade of the New Zealand Division come to relive them. Since there was no organised system of shell craters the Kiwis, by sections and platoons simply moved forward until they reached shell craters that were approximately the British position and settled in for the night, waiting for dawn when they would be able to obtain some idea of their surroundings.

He led his platoon out of their shell crater homes and, after some wandering, nay staggering around in the dark, hardly able to will one foot to follow the other he finally found Calgary Grange where he was given directions to Kansas Cross and where, he was told he would be directed to Battalion Headquarters and the rest of the Battalion.

Battalion Headquarters was a luxuriously deep shell crater into the side of which two stout planks had been driven. These provided seating accommodation for the Colonel and his staff. Whilst they sat with their feet in water, at least their backsides were kept reasonably dry. The depth was such that enemy machine gun bullets whistled harmlessly overhead.

Before first light the depleted Battalion began their march down the Wieltj-Ypres Road. Dawn found them about a mile down the road where they were met by the cookers, brought up as near as was deemed to be safe. Daylight revealed groups of leaning, sprawling scarecrows, soaked through, covered in mud, dressed in rags and with at least four days growth of beard, all minus items of clothing and equipment but all armed, gulping hot tea and ravenously devouring thick cold bacon sandwiches.

It was then that the enemy laid down a ferocious area barrage around the Stroombeek and Calgary Grange .Everyone's gaze turned towards the place they had only recently left as the area exploded in an orgy of spouts of mud, smoke and the orange flashes of exploding 5.9 inch shells, faces that expressed both relief and pity. Relief that they had escaped this maelstrom only just in time, pity for those poor devils who were still up there.

Another six miles, passing through Ypres in single file and they reached their 'Rest Billets' outside Vlamertinghe. Here they spent three nights sleeping in Nissan Huts. Then they moved on to a tented camp near Winnezeele where the living conditions were almost as bad as the front line, There they were to stay for two weeks trying to rebuild the battalion before the Brigade was ordered back into the line. Once this order came, they enjoyed the luxury of being transported by commandeered London buses to within a five mile march of Ypres. From there they made a night march into Ypres, spending the night in the peacetime Regular Belgium Army Infantry Barracks. These had been so solidly built that, in spite of the constant artillery fire that Ypres had suffered they still offered excellent accommodation. So here they enjoyed a night's sleep on beds consisting of a wooden frame across which chicken wire had been attached.

The following night they marched in silent single file out of Ypres and out to the Zillebeke road to occupy positions on the forward slopes of the Broodsiende ridge in front of the village of Zillebeke. The Battalion front extended from the Broodsiende / Zillebeke road to Molenaarelsthoek with two depleted companies of two platoons each in a line of posts, and with two companies in support some six hundred yards further back, behind the village cemetery. Battalion Head Quarters was in the Moulin Farm pill box.

The front line posts consisted of shell holes, each occupied by five or six men. The posts were under the direct observation of the enemy from the Keilburg Spur. Movement was only possible at night. It was useless trying to dig the shell holes deeper as they only filled with water and trying to make them larger only attracted the enemy snipers. In any case, any attempt at digging only resulted in disturbing decomposing dead bodies. No fires could be lit or hot food brought up from behind due to the difficulties encountered by carrying parties trying to negotiate such a sea of mud. Water was scarce and the only chance of a hot drink depended on the possession of a Tommy's cooker'. Fierce fighting was still going on to the north of them at Passchendaele but the condition of the ground in front of their positions made an enemy attack unlikely. Nevertheless, enemy snipers were constantly busy.

Each night, after dark he would go with great caution between each of the other seven posts that contained his platoon. He would then crawl to the shell hole that was Company headquarters and make his daily report, usually returning with whatever Company H.Q. had been able to acquire. These would usually be tins of 'Bully Beef and full water bottles to distribute among his platoon.

After four days, the support companies moved up to relieve them whilst they moved back into the support positions. Here, at least life was a little more relaxed. They were no longer bothered by snipers but the shelling was both incessant and accurate. Zonnebeke and the Zonnebeke Road were places to avoid.

After a further four days of this troglodyte existence the Battalion was relieved and went back as reserve in the dark warrens which were the ramparts. Here at least they were safe from shelling, although working parties outside the ramparts were required each day. Here awaited him that most glorious of all things: MAIL. There was a whole bundle from her, a number written in the top left hand corner to indicate the order in which they should be read. How did she find so much to write about, always something new, always about a golden future that awaited them? Never about the war. As always he read and reread her letters in numerical order as if they were a novel. In addition there were some five letters from his Mum.

On the second day out of the line he was summoned by the Colonel who told him "Colonel Baxter has requested your return to his Battalion. I don't want to lose you, particularly at this time but he seems very anxious for your return. Have you any comments to make? He replied "Whilst I would be sad to leave my platoon, I would like to return to Colonel Baxter's battalion if at all possible sir. After all, his Battalion is where I began." The Colonel, clearly not too pleased replied "Well, I see your point. Very well then, so be it." Two days later saw him hitching a ride in a Lorry, bound for St.Omer. From there by train to Rouen where he had a boring wait while the Railway Transport Officer located the Battalion and arranged his onward journey. After what seemed an age he was told that the Battalion was out of the line and resting near Arras. Therefore he was to travel on a train bound for Amiens where Motor Transport would be arranged to meet him and transport him to the Battalion.

He finally reached the Battalion and presented himself to the Adjutant, the same officer who had led them out of the line after the Somme, who greeted him warmly and said "It's wonderful to see you again old boy but you look done in. You're sweating like a blown horse. Are you all right?" He had to admit. "I think I'm running a temperature sir, I've got a stinking headache and my legs and back feel as though someone has laid into me with a pick axe handle. It came on during the motor journey, a scotch and an aspirin will probably fix it." The Adjutant replied "Aspirin be damned.You're seeing the M.O."

The Medical Officer didn't take long to decide what his problem was, saying "You young man are suffering from Trench Fever. In addition to which you have an infected sore in your right ankle. It's hospital for you"

In 1917 Trench Fever was an ailment not properly understood. It is a moderately serious disease caused by the bites of body lice that have become infected be the excreta of body lice .It has an incubation period of about two weeks followed by a fever of five days or more. The onset of symptoms are a sudden high fever, sever headache, pain in moving the eyeballs, soreness in leg and back muscles and extremely sensitive shins. Recovery usually takes over month. During the First World War it infected the armies fighting in Flanders, France. Poland, Galicia, Italy, Salonika Macedonia and Mesopotamia. In the Second World War the Germany Armies in Russia were to suffer badly from the disease.

So, much to his delight, fever not withstanding he found himself on a Hospital train bound for Etaple. However, his joyful anticipation of being reunited with her was short lived. On arrival at No.23 General Hospital he was examined by a Canadian Doctor who held the rank of Major and who, through his young view of life seemed to be a rather elderly father figure, confirmed the diagnosis of the Battalion M.O. and advised him that he was destined for Blighty. The Major only smiled at his protestations and pleadings to remain at Etaple saying "You're the first patient to pass through my hands who didn't want to go to Blighty. Do I detect some personal agenda, a member of our nursing staff perhaps? But our role here is the treatment of battle casualties which you are not There is no doubt that you are sick but I cannot have this hospital cluttered with patients who could be treated elsewhere. So, I am sorry young man but you are going back on tonight's Hospital train to Boulogne and hence to England."

So, although one of the staff promised tell to her how he had passed through the Base Hospital 23 and of his failure to remain , twenty four hours later found him in a Hospital near Guildford, really a commandeered "Stately Home 'the property, he was told of one Lady Horton. Here his routine became hot baths, bandages and kaolin poultices for his infected ankle, followed by more hot baths. Most wonderful of all was the luxury of clean sheets.

After about one week he was up and about, enjoying walks with other patients around the gardens, even occasionally accompanied by the Lady Horton, none less. Lady Horton had a strong belief in the spirit world and in reincarnation and would assure all those she accompanied that the Allied dead, now in the great by and by were willing the allies to fight on and win for, she would say 'they know our cause to be just' She was, however, a bit miffed when one patient asked her "Are the German dead in 'the great by and by' willing their side on to win?" Her Ladyship was not impressed by such a question.

Finally he was granted ten days "Sick Leave" which he was able to spend in his home and which fell over the Christmas holiday. He arrived at his home in the late afternoon of Christmas Eve bearing a turkey that he had bought from a 'Barrow Boy' who was vending outsider Kings Cross Station and a bottle of Port, which his mother insisted could not be opened until the Christmas dinner. When it was eventually opened the following day after their traditional meal, his mother sampled a glass, probably the first for a long time; she had an uncontrollable fit of the giggles, interspaced with "it's gone to my head! In later life, he realized that whilst the Port may have 'gone her head' , the giggles were more likely a visible sign of relief from the terrible worry and anxiety which she endured every minute of her life while her son was away at the front and in harms way. But that was something that only life could teach him.

The following day he joined his Brother –in- Law at the local pub, 'The Quarryman's Arms' for a long chat and to enjoy a pint of beer. During this pleasant hour he heard a local voice, speaking of him to his companion say "'Yon (he or 'him over there') thinks ee's (he's) good!" an expression common in Yorkshire meaning 'he has ideas above his station!". He smiled, thinking to himself "I had some men in my platoon who thought as that bloke does. But no longer. !"

He did pay a visit to her parents, shortly before the end of his ten days to wish them a 'Happy New Year' – it seemed inappropriate to wish them a Merry Christmas! They were, as usual warm and friendly and, in fact asked him if he and his family had a nice Christmas, which was something to add to his education. They told him that they had received a letter from their daughter in which she expressed her sorrow at not seeing him when he transited Etaple.

Before his leave was complete he received a telegram saying that, before returning to France he was to attend an "Officers' training course" which, it appeared he should have, but had not attended before. So, leave complete he reported to the Guards Depot at Pirbright. The course was, clearly intended for 'Would be' officers, not for a subaltern with a wound stripe and a Military Medal ribbon. So, it was decided that his course would be abbreviated and, instead of being chased around Pirbright parade ground by some fearsome looking old 'Dug out' R.S.M. he would be instructed on 'So called' "Mess Etiquette", how to pass the port and on 'How to call upon the Colonel's Lady' all of which struck him as being a complete waste of time. Finally an end came to his course and he was instructed to report to the Transport Office in Southampton docks where he would take charge of a draft bound for his battalion.

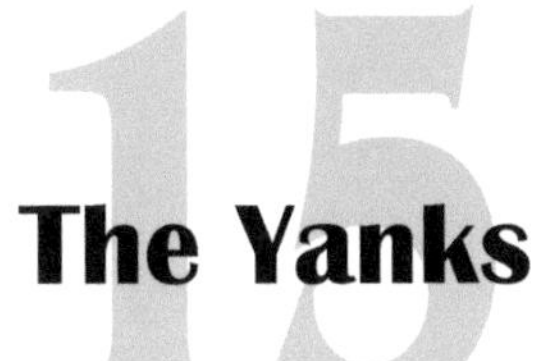

The Yanks

Over there, say a prayer,
We're coming over,
And we won't come back
'Till it's over, over there

Popular song

Southampton Docks were teeming with American soldiers, tall men of good physique and with close cropped hair who saluted him with a curios salute formed by a half cupped hand, accompanied by a smile and a friendly "'morning Sur" or 'morning Loo-tenant" .They were, he gathered passing through Southampton on their way to Le Havre. All seemed to be in their mid twenties. And it was here that he experienced his first personal encounter when he asked an American Major for directions to the Office of the British Rail Transport Officer. It transpired that this Officer, one Major Fielding was the U.S.Army equivalent of an R.T.O. whose job was to arrange a smooth transfer of men into France. Hearing that his transport to Dieppe was not scheduled to leave the docks until early evening the Major insisted that he join them for lunch in their 'Officers' Club', a nearby requisitioned house. Here he was introduced to the Major's staff and to a number of younger and junior officers who were in transit. A place was found for him at their table, then there was put before him a sirloin steak with fried egg on top, 'French Fries', which, he discovered is what they called chipped potatoes and a salad. A meal like he had never eaten before. This was followed by Apple pie smothered in ice cream. There was no alcohol served with the meal, instead a coffee that matched the meal and which was available in copious quantities.

He found his hosts to be polite, unpretentious, and with great enthusiasm for their profession and for their army. Enthusiasm the likes of which he had not seen in his own army since the Somme. They explained to him that the peacetime strength of the U.S.Army was only 100,000 men, a third of which were cavalry, but President Wilson had asked Congress to provide funds to build an army of four million men with a field army of two million soldiers of all arms. The

President had decreed that the most democratic way to raise an army was by conscription, which they called “the Draft” Remembering the thousands of idealistic young men, many of them his friends, he had to agree.

They explained to him that initially, to save shipping space only men were crossing the Atlantic .They were to be equipped with British and French arms but soon their home industries would have reached their full potential and then they would use weapons of their own design. They had many questions to ask him about trench warfare, about the British and French armies, and about British equipment, especially about the Short Lee Enfield rifle. Why, they asked was not this rifle fitted with a firing sling, like their own home grown Springfield? When he said that he had no experience of using a firing sling, they went to a great deal of trouble to explain the advantages which he promised he would try out as soon as he was back with his Battalion. They asked him many questions about the Lewis gun, which caused him to express some surprise since he understood that it was of American design. Major Fielding explained that, yes the weapon had been designed by an American, one Colonel Lewis but in 1913 the design was rejected by the U.S.Army. Such was Colonel Lewis’s frustration that he resigned his commission and set sail for Europe where he sold a manufacturing licence to the Belgium Government. The British Company ‘Birmingham Small Arms’ also bought a licence to manufacture the gun for the British Army. Now, belatedly the U.S. Army had ordered a version firing U.S.Army standard 0.30 calibre rimless ammunition which would be manufactured in the States. In the meantime, they would be using the British version which fired 0.303 calibre rounds. Hence the interest.

When he commented on the age of their soldiers they explained that the U.S. Army only accepted recruits of twenty four to thirty years of age and who were of good physique. This at a time when the British army consisted of men in the age bracket of eighteen to forty years. When he told them that his official age, as far as the army were concerned was twenty two but in actual fact he had only recently celebrated his twentieth birthday and that the Army was still accepting under age boys who falsified their date of birth, his hosts were astounded.

This experience brought home to him the size, the power and the industrial strength of America. He was also impressed by the casual attitude which his hosts had shown towards the mammoth tasks in building the field army that was planned They had much to ask about the possibility of "Breaking Out" and conducting 'open warfare where the rifle would be the dominant weapon, rather than the grenade. He agreed with their view but pointing out that first one had to break through the enemy's fortifications before a "Break-out" could be achieved. The Germans, he reminded them were a formidable enemy, very good soldiers who, no doubt were determined not to permit a "Breakout", adding that whilst he agreed with their comments about the rifle, it was not really a suitable weapon with which to dislodge a determined enemy armed with a machine gun in a concrete bunker.

One Officer asked "Could he help him with a problem they had encountered?"

He told him how they had tried to obtain a consignment of toilet paper from the British Army supply channels they were supposed to deal through but had failed. In fact they had resolved the problem by a direct purchase from a Southampton based wholesaler. Future supplies would come directly from the States. "Why" they asked "is this such a problem?". Without thinking carefully about his answer, he replied "The British Army do not supply toilet paper", and then wished he'd tried to find a more diplomatic way of putting it. His Hosts all looked at him in astonishment. "But how" they asked "do your men keep themselves clean?" Knowing that, in his army this problem demanded a great deal of improvisation ranging from the use of newspapers, old letters, grass. straw, empty sand bags or sometimes not at all, the only reply that he could muster was "With great difficulty!" This brought forth laughter which enabled the conversation to move onto another subject. But it told him something about the attitudes that prevailed in his army compared with another.

Finally he had to ask to be excused for he still had to locate the draft that he was supposed to command. But his hosts were not finished with him. They presented him with five pounds of ground Columbian coffee beans and a box of fifty "King Edward" cigars, their gift to the "Officers Club" of his Battalion; In addition there was a large packet of beef sandwiches which would sustain him during his voyage across the channel. In fact there was, in his opinion enough food in the parcel to sustain a platoon.

Later, sitting alone he thought about the more relaxed but clearly efficient way these Americans went about their business compared with the way the British Army went about theirs. Perhaps there was a better way of doing things. But what, he thought, will these men be like after three years of war. Will they have the same tired, nerve racked look that many British and French troops now had?

But he was not alone in being in awe at the strength available to the elbow of President Woodrow Wilson,

He found the Battalion out of the line resting near Amiens, preparing to go back into the line. First he was interviewed by Colonel Baxter who had many questions to ask him, about old friends, about Passchendael and about the brief 'Officer Training Course' that he had attended. The Colonel roared with laughter on hearing his tale of the lecture on 'How to visit the Colonel's Lady', assuring him that 'His missus was a Scots Lassie who would have no interest in such Bull'. Finally he told him "You're going back to your old Company as a platoon commander. There are a few old faces but many new ones, mainly conscripts but we strive hard to keep the spirit of a Kitchener Battalion.

His welcome into the Officers Mess was warm and friendly, particularly from his company commander who assured him that 'I'm glad to have you back'

16 Operation Michael

And then the Officer will meet you.
With a tot of rum he'll greet you
And he'll say "Mate, retaliate,
With a Mills ' Number five"

Sergeant Albert Sands. 1915

Chief of the German General Staff, Erich Von Ludendorff addressing a conference of army commanders is reported to have said "Our overall position requires the earliest possible blow, if possible at the end of February or at the beginning of March before the Americans can throw strong forces onto the scales" With an extra forty four divisions released from the eastern front, following the collapse of the Russian Army he believed he had the strength to achieve his objective. The plan was that the first blow would fall on the weakest sector of the British line between Arras and St.Quentin, over the old Somme battlefields.

It was here that ,at 0400 hours on March 21st 1918 , after a short bombardment and aided by a dense morning mist squads of German storm troopers slipped across no-mans land, bypassing strong points and seeking weaknesses in the British line, leaving the mopping up to be done by support formations. British defences were caught completely off balance but, although the line bent, it did not break.

March 1918 found the Battalion again resting near Arras after a spell in the line. On the morning of the 21st, while he and his fellow officers were finishing breakfast, a Signaller entered the mess, walked up to Colonel Baxter, saluted smartly and handed him a slip of paper. The Colonel studied the paper carefully, in fact he appeared to read it twice, then said "Thank you, please acknowledge receipt". Then he rose to his feet and tapped the side of his plate to gain attention. When all had fallen silent, he said "Gentlemen, we have orders from Brigade to be ready to move in six hours time. In fact the whole Division is under orders. I suggest that you do not linger over breakfast but go to your companies now. The Adjutant and I have much to do. When we know more, I shall call an Officers' Meeting. Thank you." For a moment, there was a stunned silence, then much scraping of chairs as everyone left the mess in great haste.

They detrained at Marcelclave where, of all things a fleet of London Omnibuses awaited them. These took them to a point west of Villers Carbonnelles where they debussed, dumped their heavy packs and peeled down into 'Battle Order'. Now they were led by a Lieutenant and two men who were clearly exhausted and who walked as if in a daze. Their unit had been retreating for three days and clearly had been badly mauled. From these exhausted remnants they took over, forming a screen along the embankment of a sunken section of the Villers Carbonnellers - Barleux road whilst these gallant survivors staggered back to the Omnibuses that were to take them to where the Battalion had only recently en bussed.

Colonel Baxter's orders were to form a screen across the advancing enemy's front whilst the rest of the division formed a strong defensive line to his rear.

Scouts were sent out who returned to report that the enemy were about a mile and a half ahead but, apart from taking a few pot shots at them, they seemed, for the time being at least, to be more interested in looting a British Y.M.C.A canteen. The Colonel elected to form a line consisting of three company strong points each covering the other two and with a fourth company held in support. Each strong point would consist of three platoon posts with one platoon in support.

As they were taking up positions, Colonel Baxter overheard two men having a grouse saying 'This will be another fucking staff fuck up' The Colonel rounded on them, saying 'If you fellows cannot come into action without using that kind of language, then damn you. Clear off, go back with the transport and clean latrines and leave the line to better men!" The men apologised and continued to their position. The Kitchener Battalion spirit prevailed indeed

So now they waited. His platoon was on the right flank of his company which was, in fact the right flank of the Battalion. He positioned his Lewis Gun team where they could sweep with enfilade fire any formation approaching the platoon front. During the night the transport caught up with them, bringing corned beef sandwiches, jam and rum plus an extra bandolier of one hundred rounds per man.

Dawn came cold and damp and they watched their enemy form up behind a hedge. Many shivered, not only from the cold morning air.

Then they came on, shouting 'Hoch Hoch, Hoch!' The platoon wag said in a loud clear voice "Hock Hock Hock! I thought that was a bleedin' drink!" Nervous, infectious laughter rang out throughout the platoon, relieving some of the tension. When the range was down to six hundred yards the entire Battalion opened rapid fire, cutting the first and then the second wave to pieces. Now their enemy withdrew to the cover from which they had started, and from where a coloured very light rose into the sky as they requested artillery support. Soon black woolly air burst appeared above them which emitted long seeking fingers of grey shrapnel balls. But their firing was desultory, the enemy artillery having had trouble keeping up with their infantry and the ranging was inaccurate, either long and ripping into the ground behind them or short and tearing into the enemy wounded who littered the ground before the Battalion's positions.

Now their enemy seemed content to engage them with small arms fire. Colonel Baxter realised that the intention was to keep him believing that another wave would soon be thrown against his line whilst his enemy tried to get around his flanks, leaving other formations to mop up his battalion. Therefore he elected to frustrate their plan by conducting a fighting withdrawal to another position to the rear.

The Battalion was now ordered to disengage from the enemy and fall back onto Soyecourt where they arrived at 01:00AM. At 10:00AM Colonel Baxter was ordered to take his Battalion back to hold a line near the Railway Station. Here, again Colonel Baxter employed his technique of a front line consisting of three company strong points with one company in support, each of a series of three platoon posts with one platoon in support. Each post or strong point covering the other strong points or posts.

The enemy persued his usual strategy of seeking weaknesses by way of probing attacks but now their follow up attacks were preceded by howitzer and trench mortar barrages which were intense and accurate. The Battalion began to take very sobering casualties and soon was forced to fall back, holding a line parallel to the railway line. His platoon, now reduced to little more than a section in strength received some welcome reinforcement from a Sapper Corporal, a Cornish man named Pendragon and four Sappers who, the Corporal told him were all that was left of his Section. He said his Royal Engineers Company had been thrown into the line as infantry and had lost some 70% of its strength, including all their Officers. Corporal Pendragon was to prove that he had the fighting spirit of a Tiger. The attacks, including the artillery fire intensified. Units became scattered and he soon realized that he had lost contact with the rest of the Company and that he was being attacked on both flanks as the enemy tried to get behind him. His platoon was now reduced to a handful of men including some wounded, albeit walking wounded. Clearly these men would soon either be dead or be 'rounded up' as prisoners. So, remembering the adage about 'those who live to fight another day' he decided that his men would slip away in pairs and try to contact the rest of the Battalion whilst he and Corporal Pendragon covered their withdrawal with the platoon Lewis gun. As soon all had made good their retreat he and the Corporal loaded the last full drum onto the Lewis gun and began their own withdrawal, Corporal Pendragon leading and carrying the Lewis gun, he following with both their rifles.

They had reached the shelter of a sunken road which, they hoped would lead them to freedom when three German soldiers stepped out of cover, rifles levelled, blocking their way. Corporal Pendragon, seeing them first, swung the gun towards them, presumably intending to fire the gun from the hip but he was felled by a shot which appeared to hit him in the temple. The Germans stepped towards him, three rifles pointed at him, expressions telling him that they would happily use them and indicated that he should drop his weapons and raise his hands. Seeing no profit in dieing a needless death he did as they commanded. Following a punch in the chest from a rifle butt and another in the mouth from a fist he was frisked for other weapons. One of his captures picked up the Lewis gun, whooped with delight and asked him, via sign language 'where were the spare drums?' This was a weapon which the Germans held in high esteem, calling it the Belgium rattlesnake 'He replied "Kaput". Whether this was the correct response he never knew. It certainly was not the response that had been hoped for because it earned him another punch, this time in the ear, which made his ear drums ring. Then he was marched away to an area where a number of British prisoners had been assembled, probably about three hundred. Here he was searched, his wrist watch taken from him although they did not discover a map which he had stuffed inside his tunic. Since he was wearing the uniform of a private soldier his captors assumed that was what he was. He chose not to enlighten them. They indicated that he should join the others. After a while they were marched down the road, over the ridge and into what was now the German rear area where they were handed over to a group of older soldiers, men probably in their late forties, even early fifties who seemed ancient in the eyes of someone, like him in his early twenties. One of the guards who spoke English and who said he had worked in London before the war told them that they were fed up with the war and that, because of the blockade by the British Navy people in Germany were starving. He also said that there would not be rations for them and that they would have to survive on what they could scavenge.

The German rear area was a hive of activity. Coming up the road was a stream of lorry borne German infantry who were in high spirits and who shouted abuse and insults at them, calling them 'Englisher schwine' and words in German that he could not understand. Many of the Lorries had inscriptions chalked on the sides which their elderly guards told them read 'On to Paris'.

Soon they were put to work burying the German dead. No effort was made to identify these corpses, they were simply dropped into open graves as fast as these could be dug so, needless to say when the attention of their guards was elsewhere they searched these dead for any food and for water bottles before they were interred.

As night began to fall they were marched to a deserted farm and herded into a cow shed. A supply of dry straw was provided for them to sleep on. For the next three days they were awakened at dawn each morning, given a small piece of black bread and a tin of weak coffee and then marched out on a work detail repairing the shell damaged roads. Their scavenging for food and drink became less and less fruitful. Anything that looked edible was collected even, on one occasion some brown shelled snails. Their diet was hardly suitable for hard physical labour and many of his fellow prisoners began to look old and haggard. Then many began to contract dysentery, followed soon by vomiting and sever dehydration and then death. They buried their comrades where ever they could, making sure to leave the dog tags with the bodies to enable some future identification and using whatever material they could find to manufacture grave markers.

From his experience of trench warfare he knew how serious the Medical Corps people regarded dysentery, which it was a highly contagious sickness and that isolation of the sick was extremely important if the sickness was not to spread. For this reason, although hygiene in the trenches was a joke, nevertheless he knew that maintenance of latrines was regarded as extremely important. He tried to convince the English speaking guard of this danger, asking for fresh water for the sick to fight against dehydration, that the sick should be segregated and that they should be given an opportunity to dig extra latrines He only replied "We cannot give you what we do not have, As for time to dig latrines, I have my orders". It was this that made him realise that if he was not to die, he must escape.

At night he lay awake and, in his mind made many plans to escape. The first one concerned a German observation balloon which was tethered near by and which they passed each morning as they were marched off to work. He confided his plan with two others. Under cover of darkness they would break out of their cow shed prison and reach the Balloon, clamber into the basket, cut the mooring ropes and, once airborne let it drift over the lines to the British positions. He even stole a pair of wire cutters which he saw laying around unattended and smuggled them back into the farm. With these he would cut the mooring ropes and drift away to freedom. But it occurred to him that he would need a favourable wind and, having got his balloon airborne he would need to know how to persuade it to descend back to earth. Also he would need to know how to navigate it. With the fighting now very fluid he hardly wanted to land his balloon amongst its rightful owners, so he abandoned his plan of escape via a balloon flight. His next plan was to break out alone and hide himself in the country side. Then, moving at night he would pass through the enemy lines and reach his own people. Here the difficulty would be he would need a portable supply of food and drink on which to sustain himself throughout his journey. To this end he started to squirrel away a reserve of food. This was difficult because food was already in short supply.

However, before he could finalize a plan things began to change. Clearly there was a lot of activity at the front. In the far distance they began to hear the sound of heavy gun fire and long columns of lorry borne German infantry began to stream back down the roads on which they worked. Lorries full of men no longer jubilant. Exhausted men whose haggard faces reminded him of his own battalion after the Somme.

A few days passed then, one afternoon after completing their 'road repair' task, instead of returning to the old farm they were marched to a railway siding and ordered into some Goods Cars. Here they were to spend the night, guarded by their elderly guards. It was during their entraining that the Guard who spoke English heard one of his fellow prisoners address him as 'Sir'. "Why does he call you Sir?" he asked "Are you an Officer?" He replied "No, he's being sarcastic. He thinks I'm 'Bossy!' The Guard smiled and said "I see" but his expression suggested that he didn't believe him.

Here they were to remain until the following morning. Not the most comfortable night he was to experience.

Just after sunrise the train began to move but, after about thirty minutes they were strafed by three British fighter planes. The train stopped and the Driver and his Fireman together with the Guards jumped down onto the track and sought cover on the embankment. Seeing this as his opportunity he slid open the unlocked door of the Goods Car just far enough to slide out and dropped onto the track, climb between the wheels and lie face down between the rails, hoping and praying that, first of all he had not been seen and that, when the train moved off no piece of coupling was hanging down far enough to decapitate him.

The Train Crew returned with the Guards who only made a brief perfunctory check of their charges, cursing them because the wagon doors were open and slamming them shut with threats as to what would happen if they were opened again. He, pushing himself, especially his face as far as it would go into the ballast like an Ostrich, buttocks clenched tight with fear, trying not to breath, not to make a sound, Soon the train moved off and, after what seemed an age it had passed over him. He lay perfectly still between the rails until the train had passed out of sight. Then he made a quick dash for some thick bushes on the embankment and hid himself until the light failed. Now, advancing with great caution he headed into the setting sun and to where he thought he would find the allied lines. When it became too dark to be sure of his heading, rather than wander off his course he settled down in a copse, ate his piece of bread and tried to sleep.

At first light he spotted a farm, about two miles away. This was where he headed, hoping to be able to steal some food. Reaching the out buildings he watched from behind a tree but no one seemed to be about. Throwing caution to the wind he slipped into a barn and hid himself in some hay in the loft. A dog began to bark but stopped when a human voice cursed it and demanded silence.

About mid day his curiosity was aroused by the grunting and squealing of pigs. Looking through a gap in the barn wall he observed an elderly man, who he assumed must be the farmer filling the pig's trough with what appeared to be kitchen waste.

The farmer disappeared from sight and, after a while having presumably eaten their fill the pigs settled down and, apart from the odd grunt appeared to be sleeping. Now, with great caution he slipped out of the barn and made his way over to the pig trough to see what they had left. As he sorted through the swill, seeking anything that appeared edible he became aware that he was being watched. Turning slowly around he found that he was being observed by the same elderly man. He had a mop of steel grey hair, was dressed in a pale blue smock, black cotton trousers, with wooden sabots on his feet and was watching him from a distance of about twenty yards. He stood up slowly and carefully, not wanting to cause any alarm and, trying to muster his limited French, he said "*Monsieur, .je suis un officier britannique, un prisonnier de guerre.J'ai évader le Boche*" The elderly man, possibly in his seventies silently regarded him for a few moments then, jerked his head to indicate that he should follow him, turned on his heel saying *Allez!* and walked towards and into the farm house.

The kitchen contained what he was accustomed to call a kitchen range consisting of a grate, in which a small fire glowed, and to one side an oven, the other a boiler. An iron kettle or coffee pot stood on the hob. Much the same as he was accustomed to seeing in his home town. Under the window was an earthen kitchen sink with a hand pump to provide water, presumably from the farm well. A plain wooden table with four hard back kitchen chairs stood in the middle of the room.

Standing before the kitchen range with her back to the door was a dark haired well built, muscular woman, probably in her late thirties or early forties. She turned to face them, wiping the sweat from her brow with the back of her hand and regarded him with suspicion, even possibly fear. She wore a black cotton dress which fitted her closely and, despite being worn thin with age, displayed her statuesque physique to advantage. Around her head she wore a scarf, tied to hold her hair back away from her face. Her feet were bare. Her face, lined for her age suggested a life of toil. . The elderly man spoke to her in very rapid French and in a dialect that he could not follow. She replied in a way that seemed to register disapproval, for their conversation sounded somewhat argumentative but, after more words from the elderly man she shrugged her shoulders and said in what sounded like a reluctant tone *"Je suis d'accord"* The elderly man then turned to him and speaking slowly and clearly so that his French would be understood, told him that he could stay in the barn for one night but he must be gone by first light. If Le Boche were to find him there, they would shoot both he and Madam. In the meantime, Madam would feed him and give him some bread for his journey. He went on to say that the sound of gun fire was now from the North West. Therefore he suggested that the safest direction, avoiding German patrols would be South West. He said that he must leave, that he was an old man and running the farm without his son, who was away at the war, was very hard for him. Then he left the house and returned to his work about the farm.

He was not sure if Madam was his wife or the wife of his absent son.

With a shrug of her shoulder and the open palm of her hand Madam invited him to take a seat at the kitchen table. Then she placed before him a meal of cold pork sausages, bread and hot coffee which he devoured with great relish. Madam sat on the opposite side of the table, lit a strong smelling cigarette and watched him eat with interest. When he finished his meal and pushed back his chair, already feeling a new man. She offered him one of her cigarettes which he accepted, lighting it from the match struck and offered in her cupped hand, her now confident dark eyes regarded him with great interest, her lips showing a suggestion of a smile. On drawing the smoke into his lungs he choked, spluttered and coughed, much to her amusement. Something about her reminded him of the higher class of woman he had seen in Egypt, women who returned the admiring looks of British soldiers with a contemptuous glare. Perhaps it was her incredibly dark eyes that stared confidently at him through the smoke of her cigarette. Searching his memory for a suitable thing to say he asked her *"vous étés une Arabe Madame? "* She smiled at his schoolboy if not soldier French and replied *"No Monsieur, je suis Torque"*

Feeling that the only thing he needed to complete his contentment was to be clean he asked *"Je me laverais? "* When this produced a puzzled expression maybe because, clearly she did not understand his attempt at French, particularly when spoken with the flat vowels of a Yorkshire accent he made gestures which, he hoped would convey the impression of some one washing. When she finally understood his request, her expression turning to smile she said *"Ahh! oui"*. Then she squeezed her nose between her right thumb and for finger, wafted the palm of her left hand across her face, indicating that his aroma was not exactly desirable and replied *"Oui, d'accord!"* Getting up from her chair she indicated that he should remove his tunic and shirt and follow her to the earthen sink. Once there she took him by the nape of his neck with one hand and with a strength that surprised him, pushed his head under the pump, and with her other hand worked the pump handle to send a flood of cold water into his hair. Then she proceeded to rub strong smelling soap into it and rub and rub and rub, continually rinsing with one cold deluge after another from the pump. This completed, she removed the kettle from the hob and filled a shaving mug with hot water, produced a shaving brush and open razor and indicated that he should take a seat. Working up a soapy lather into his whiskers she proceeded to shave the grimy beard from his face. This completed, she combed back his still wet hair with a brush that he thought was probably intended to groom horses and, using the open razor trimmed it back to a more presentable length. After filling a wooden tub with pump water, she placed it on the kitchen floor, handed him the soap and a towel and indicated that he should wash himself all over, watching him strip with the eye of a connoisseur. Seemingly satisfied with his washing she picked up his long johns between her right thumb and fore finger and, with a *'Voila!'*, disdainfully tossed them onto the kitchen fire. Collecting his shirt, socks and boots from the floor she disappeared into another room. She returned carrying a pair of wooden sabots, a darned but clean pair of long johns, darned but clean socks, a worn but clean grey flannel shirt and a round loaf of bread. She watched him towel himself dry and dress in much the way, he felt, that a tiger would watch a tethered goat. Then, having established that the sabots fitted his feet she added to her gifts a wicked looking clasp knife and a small flask which contained, she whispered, knitting her eyebrows into a scowl, pursing her lips and glancing towards the door 'Calvados.' He knew Calvados to be an apple Brandy and that many farmers owned stills from which they produced their own supply, a source that had a fearsome reputation. Her discreet gesture seemed to suggest that this item was not on the list of supplies approved by the elderly farmer. Possibly it was from his private stock. So he expressed his thanks silently, his lips mouthing *Merci*.

Then she departed. His boots and his shirt were, he concluded the bill for their hospitality. He slipped the clasp knife into his trouser pocket, the flask into the breast pocket of his tunic, vowing to himself that this would be used only in emergency.

Now he retired to the barn, climbed into the hay loft and snuggled down into the straw feeling, for once that not only was his appetite satisfied he also felt clean for the first time in some weeks, a feeling he would never forget. Soon he was asleep.

Like a hunted animal, one never sleeps deeply in such circumstance and, during the night something disturbed him. He sat up and listened, sensing that he was not alone in the hay loft. Then, peering through the gloom he realised his visitor was not a German patrol but Madam, standing before him. Putting her extended fore finger to her pursed lips, telling him that he must not make a sound she crossed her forearms, reached down for the hem of her flannel night dress, lifted it over her head , dropped it onto the straw and stood before him, quite naked. Then, kneeling at his side she pushed him onto his back into the straw. After her brief preliminary titivation, which made him gasp, first with surprise but then with sheer ecstasy, she pressed her cheek against his and whispered, in a voice tinged with yearning - even sadness, *Baise – Moi!*. Then she bestrode him, kneeling across his hips in the way that one would mount a pony. For the next hour or so she introduced him to forms and variations in the art of love that he would never forget. Finally, bending over him, she kissed him one last time, whispered '*Bonne Chance*' into his ear, picked up her night dress and disappeared from the hay loft as silently and as swiftly as a wraith.

He awoke to the call of the farm yard cock shortly before dawn.

Pushing his toes into his new Sabots he donned his tunic, picked up his supplies, slipped out of the barn and was gone. Using the rising sun as a compass and bearing in mind the advice of the elderly man he set himself a course towards a feature on the landscape which, he considered would take him west south west. After covering about four miles he reached a small copse. Now the sun was up so he decided that it was here that he would take a rest and eat some of his bread by way of breakfast. Thinking of the nights experience he recalled the comment that Squire Jones had made and thought to himself.' Yes, you were right Squire my old friend; an older woman can teach a young man many things!' He smiled to himself at the memory of his dead comrade and what he would have said if he was here beside him. Then, 'how' he thought 'would he explain himself to his girl?'. After all, he had been disloyal to her?' After a moments reflection he concluded "Well, I don't know if I will get out of this alive, so perhaps I should cross that bridge when I reach it. But there again, she will be able to enjoy the fruits of my 'Further education!' "

Using the rising sun as his compass each morning he set himself a course by selecting a feature in the landscape which he considered was a heading of south west. He estimated that, travelling with caution he was probably covering some eight miles each day but allowing for detours to avoid populated areas or areas where German troops might be found the distance covered in a straight line was probably about five miles, maybe less. And, of course he had no means of fixing his actual position. He tried to lay up each evening near a source of food with which he could supplement his fast diminishing loaf. One evening a field containing a crop of potato, another evening the crop was turnips. He was to learn that the human body soon became accustomed to lack of food but never a lack of water. He became more and more concerned about the sound of gunfire that no longer seemed to be coming from the north west but was shifting round to the south. After the fourth day he became more and more aware of increasing troop activity which demanded greater caution.

On the fifth day, as he neared the crest of a ridge he was spotted by a German patrol some five hundred yards distant. He made a bolt for it but they opened fire, several bullets buzzed past him with the sound of bees, then a hard blow bowled his legs from under him and he fell to the ground. He lay perfectly still, feigning death. Two more rounds buzzed past his head, one clipping his right ear. Then, probably assuming that they had killed him and having other fish to fry the patrol lost interest in him and moved on. As soon as he was sure he was alone, he dragged himself into the cover of some scrub and, taking out Madam's clasp knife he cut away the legs of his trousers so as to inspect his wounds. One round had hit his right thigh behind the knee, passed through his leg, fortunately without damaging any bone, and ploughed a furrow across the top of his left thigh. Cutting the water proof packet which contained his first aid kit from the flap of his jacket, he opened it and removed the shell dressing and the phial of iodine, only to find that the latter was all but empty. So he removed the flask of brandy from the breast pocket of his tunic. First he poured brandy through the hole in his right thigh, biting his lip against the sharp stinging sensation this caused, anxious not to make any noise, then he swabbed some brandy into the furrow in his left thigh. This done, he cut the shell dressing bandage in half and used the half with the shell dressing pad attached to bind the wound on his right leg. The other half he used to bind the furrow on his left leg but not before cutting a small piece from the end which he soaked in brandy. His ear felt as though he'd been stung by a wasp but since he could not inspect this wound he elected not to touch it with his dirty hands for fear of infection. Instead he satisfied himself by draping over the wound the piece of brandy soaked dressing. Then he drank the remains of the brandy, lifting the flask in salute to Madam before lying back to rest and try to recover some strength.

As the light began to fail he struggled to his feet and tried to move on. Progress was slow; his legs had both stiffened considerably, although he was able to cut a staff from a fallen sapling, which helped. As he approached a copse in which he hoped to lay up for the night a voice called out softly from cover, in English but with an American accent 'Halt' then 'Come forward with your hands up'. Then 'Far enough, Identify yourself ' He replied "I'm a British Officer. I need to get back to my Battalion". The voice now said 'Stay there. Move an' yer dead' Then the voice said 'Hey Serge. there's a guy here who speaks English, looks like a hobo but says he's a limey Officer". Next he was telling his story to an American Captain who told him 'Before we talk about getting back to your battalion we'd better do something about those wounds' then, calling over his shoulder 'Get the Medics to come and take care of this guy'.

Soon, fresh dressings on his wounds he was lifted into the back of a motor ambulance and being whisked away, first to a dressing station and then further back to a hospital. A hospital, in fact operated by the American Ambulance Corps. Here he was inspected by another Doctor, then whisked away to the operating theatre and given an anaesthetic. He awoke washed, shaved; his clothes replaced by a clean night shirt and in a wonderful clean bed. Then, for the first time in some weeks he slept like a proverbial log.

He was awakened by the usual early morning bustle of a hospital ward. First a nurse sponged his face, then served him a cup of that wonderful American coffee he had been introduced to in Southampton. Then rounds by a Doctor accompanied by a senior nurse who was somewhat startled when he addressed her as 'Sister'. The Doctor told him that in the theatre they had cut away some dead flesh from around his wounds, including his right ear, hence the bandage around his head - and put in a few stitches but his wounds were clean and should soon heal although he would be bed bound for some days adding, with a smile" Your 'Brandy' antiseptic worked very well young man". He went on to say that they would advise the British Army as to his whereabouts but that he would not be going back to them until he, the Doctor considered him to be sufficiently fit to travel. In the meantime, perhaps he would like to write to his next of kin, they would see that it was posted.

Next came a breakfast of peaches followed by pancakes smothered in Maple syrup. After breakfast a nurse brought him some writing materials and told him that there was another British soldier in the 'Enlisted Men's' ward who had actually been with them for some weeks and who was soon expecting to be returned to his own army. He asked 'would she ask this soldier to pay him a visit'. Then he wrote a short note to her and to his mother, confirming that he was safe and well and another to Colonel Baxter by way of a report.

The nursing staff, mainly girls who were all American, found him a novelty, describing him as 'cute' and addressed him as 'Mr.Britisher'. Throughout his first day they brought in friends from other wards to see their prize exhibit. Many asked "Get him to say something!" He would tease them with Yorkshire expressions like " Ee by gum" which would cause his visitors to collapse in fits of giggles and make remarks like "Gee, ain't that a cute accent!" and "He calls the Senior nurse 'Sister'" "Really? .Gee, that's really cute!"

One girl asked "Would he like a spot of tea?" They were beside themselves with delight when he said he'd 'die for one' He never did convince them that the expression was 'A POT of tea, not a Spot"

That afternoon, who should walk into the ward but Corporal Pendragon, large dressings taped on both cheeks but grinning from ear to ear. The Corporal told him how he had been hit not in the temple but in the face The bullet had entered through his cheek, passing through his face, knocking out most of his back teeth and leaving a very bloody exit wound in his other cheek .This had giving his skull one hell of a jerk, which had knocked him out cold for some considerable time. Their captor's had, it seemed assumed he was dead. Otherwise they may well have seen fit to put another bullet into him.

He went on to say that he had been told that the Battalion had taken a terrible mauling but later, had been reinforced by a Battalion of the American U.S.Marine Corps. Together, these two units had made a counter attack and regained the line from which he and the Corporal had been driven, fortunately for the Corporal who had been found still unconscious and lying where he had fallen by Medics from the American Ambulance Corps. He only regained consciousness in the hospital. He expected soon to be returned to their own Army. He was more concerned about how his girl friend would react when she discovered that he had lost most of his back teeth. Thus began an association that was to endure.

His fellow patients, American Officers considerably older than he soon took him under their wings, probably encouraged to do so by the nursing staff, particularly regarding his complete lack of kit. Soon he became known as 'The kid!' Officers would sidle up to him and say, in a very confidential manner "Say kid, maybe you could use a couple of shirts. I've put on some pounds in here and these don't fit me any more". Or the gift would take the form of a couple of pairs of socks, or underwear or handkerchiefs. Even some trousers and a pair of boots. Always the reply to any objection he might raise was "Gee, don't worry. I've ordered some new ones from the Commissariat". He was to learn from one of the Nurses that the Ambulance drivers who had taken him to the Casualty Clearing Station and then to the Hospital were former members of the American Ambulance Service who had been in France supporting the French Army since 1915. They all were unpaid volunteers recruited from the Campuses of American Colleges and Universities. Their duties had required these volunteers to serve under very hazardous conditions which had cost some 150 of them their lives. Some had been awarded the French *'Croix de Guerre'* and the *'Legion of Honour'* for their gallantry. When America had entered the war the American Ambulance Service had been inducted into the U. S. Army Ambulance Corps, so now at least these 'volunteers' were being paid. It seemed that there was no limit to the generosity of these American people.

But listening to the experiences of some of his fellow patients brought him to the conclusion that the American Army was following the same seemingly heroic but futile policies which the British Army had followed two years earlier and with the same disastrous consequences.

After some days he received some mail, a letter from his mother expressing her relief that he was safe, not merely 'Missing believed killed' as the official telegram had stated. Another letter was from 'Her' saying that she had heard the news from his mother two days before his letter had reached her and telling him how relieved she was. She asked 'could he request a transfer to Etaple so that she could take care of him.

There was also a letter from Colonel Baxter thanking him for his report which had been duly entered into the 'Battalion War Diary' and advising him that he had been promoted to a full lieutenant and recommended for the addition of a Bar to his Military Medal.

Three days later there came another letter from Colonel Baxter telling him that, in accordance with current Army policy of reducing a Brigade to a strength of three Battalions that his, nay 'THEIR' Battalion was to be disbanded, its members being dispersed to other Battalions in the Regiment. Therefore, once released from Hospital he would be recalled to the Regimental Depot from where he would be posted to another Battalion. The Colonel had added a hand written note in which he said that if, when the war ended he wished to apply for a permanent commission he would have the Colonel's recommendation and backing. The Colonel added his home address, saying that 'he and his wee lassie' would always be delighted to see him.

After a couple of days he was allowed out of bed but only into a wheel chair. This did allow him the freedom of being unaccompanied when he wished to visit the 'Loo', another expression which amused his American hosts who referred to it as 'The John', even 'The Can'.

It also enabled him to propel himself to the 'Enlisted Men's' ward to visit Corporal Pendragon and enjoy a game of Dominos. When he asked the Corporal where he had found this set of Dominos, he merely tapped the side of his nose with his forefinger and smiled a roguish smile. However, this entertainment was short lived as the Corporal soon departed back to the British Army via Doullens and sick leave in the U. K.

Now, with time on his hands his thoughts turned to the possibility that he may have a future after all. Perhaps there would be a future with her, although there was the question of different religions to consider. So, he took to consulting the U. S. Army Chaplains stationed in the hospital, one Anglican, and one a Rabi , both of whom were highly amused, as were the nursing staff by his insistence of addressing each of them as 'Padre' !. The subject he most wished to discuss was marriages of mixed religions. After several deep discussions with the Rabi he felt sufficiently well armed on the matter to be able to hold his own in any future debate regarding the life that she and he would, or could have together.

Soon he graduated from the wheel chair to a pair of crutches, taking his weight on his left leg, walking around the ward and then the hospital grounds. Another ten days and he was once more on his feet although walking with the aid of a stick. Soon his U.S. Army Doctor informed him that he had now to advise the British Army that he was fit to travel. Another couple of days and a telegram arrived ordering him to report to the Railway Transport Office in Reims where further instructions would await him.

So he departed his American hosts wearing U.S.Army trousers, shirt, tie, socks and boots and his British Army tunic which had been fumigated, steam cleaned and lovingly patched and darned by the nursing staff. He carried a U.S.Army kit bag which his hosts referred to as a duffle bag and which had a shoulder strap fitted to it, making it easier to carry. It contained two spare shirts, spare socks and underwear, toilet gear and a carton of one hundred American cigarettes. Also in the bag were his sabots, a souvenir of his days 'on the run' and of other memories. One of his fellow patients said he looked undressed without headgear and presented him with a U.S.Army Officers cap.

As he left the Hospital, bound for Reimes in a U.S.Army motor truck, it seemed all his fellow patients, at least those not bed bound and many of the nursing staff had gathered around to wish him farewell. Many slapped him on the back and told him 'Be lucky kid' and 'When this is over, come and join our Army kid'. Nurses, many tearful who kissed his cheek and told him 'Don't forget to write'

At Reims Rail Station the Transport Officer instructed him to entrain for the Base Hospital at Doullens. No amount of arguing nor pleading would persuade the Railway Transport Officer to change the destination and send him to Etaple, merely repeating "I'm sorry old boy but your orders specifically state Doullens Base Hospital. Sort it out when you get there." So Doullens it was.

At Doullens Base Hospital he was assessed by a Medical Officer who told him "First you are to take ten days home leave. Then we'll reassess your fitness category. Right now you are hardly A1, needing a stick to help you walk,' adding 'Perhaps it would be a good idea if you went back to Blighty wearing a British uniform. Otherwise you will cause the Military Police much confusion.' So he acquired a Private Soldiers uniform, getting the Base Tailor to sew a lieutenants 'Pips' onto the shoulder straps. He acquired a Regimental cap badge, not the correct one but a Regimental cap badge none the less, to add to his American Field cap, which he considered to resemble the British equivalent as near as needs be. He was issued with travel documents which authorised him to travel on the Hospital Train to Dieppe there to board the next Hospital Ship bound for Dover, hence by train to Euston .A first class rail warrant which authorised him to travel Kings Cross to Milford. He also received an advance of pay and another voucher for the sum of £6:00 so that he may purchase a new officers' uniform to replace the one which was, presumably, along with the rest of his personal possessions still with the stores of his now defunct Battalion deposited in some supply depot where they would remain, no doubt for an eternity.

17
Blighty

Eytee Tiddlee Eytee
I'll be up your nightie,
Blighty is the place for me.

Soldiers' version of a popular song

So now he took train to Dieppe and joined the ship bound for Dover, a vessel with a white hull on which a number of large Red Cross's had been painted.

As the ship nosed out into the Channel it encountered a stiff swell, indicating that a storm was brewing up but his fellow passengers were not subdued as they had been when he last crossed the Channel but in the opposite direction. Now they were a light hearted crowd, full of laughter who chatted and joked, happy at the thought of 'being out of it'.

Dover Harbour was a hive of activity. Orderlies carried stretcher cases from the interior of the vessel, placed them on large perambulators and wheeled them across to the waiting Hospital Train were nurses in starched uniforms took them into their care. Walking wounded and 'Sick leave' cases such as he walked across the dock and boarded the train and found seats in compartments set aside for them... Soon they were speeding through the green fields of Kent.

Euston Station was much as he remembered it. On the opposite platform the same sad sights, wives with children, sweethearts saying good bye to loved ones. Elderly men trying to fight back tears saying good bye to sons. At least this time there were some excited faces looking for loved ones being off loaded from the Hospital train and into Ambulances which would take them to Hospitals and the hope of living. Here first he changed his Francs into pounds then, walking out into the street he took a taxi cab to Kings Cross Station, the Cabbie refusing his fare, and boarded a train for Milford.

Four hours later and he was walking across Milford town centre, buying a bunch of flowers from a Florist on the way and boarded a tram for home. Tossing his bag into the stairwell he climbed the tram stairs, to take a seat on the top deck. Lighting a cigarette he was soon soaking in all the wonderful and familiar sights. Street corners, Parks, Shops, Chapels, Churches, Pubs all filled him with the happiness that only a traveller returning after a long absence will ever appreciate.

Walking from the tram stop to the door of his home he was accompanied by local children who had barely started school when he left. Now they insisted in carrying his bag, asking him many questions such as "how many Germans have you shot?" and who gazed on him with the admiration, if not the hero worship only found in small boys. Then he was at the door. First pausing to control his own emotions he opened it calling "Mum! I'm home"

She burst out of her small kitchen, drying her hands on a tea towel and calling to one of his sisters who followed her to 'Put the kettle on', eyes filling with tears saying "Oh, Son. You should have told me you were coming" Then, reaching up to put her arms around his neck she burst into tears, saying "Thank God, oh thank God. I've been so worried".

The following morning he dressed in his civilian clothes which, three years ago his mother had bought for him, fortunately on the large side, saying that 'he would grow into them' which, in point of fact he had. First he first called at the village Post Office to mail a letter to her in which he pleaded that she should request leave so as to be with him. Then, his £6:00 voucher in his pocket he walked, with the aid of his stick, to town by way of the local park, bound for the 'Victoria and Albert Arcade' where he intended to place an order for a replacement uniform. Here he encountered the young lady who had tried, months before to present him with a white feather. She looked at him rather curiously, probably trying to recall why his face was familiar. Unable to resist the opportunity, he bowed gracefully from the hips and said "Good morning Madam. Are you going to give me a white feather?"

The young woman looked at him in astonishment and then fled as though she had seen a ghost, followed by his helpless laughter.

Finding his progress with a still 'gammy leg' limiting and tiresome he opted to finish his journey by tram. Again the conductor, after asking "Are you a wounded soldier?" refusing to take his fare.

Arriving at Victoria and Albert Arcade he opened the door of her fathers shop and walked in. Her father and his small staff all stopped what they were doing, her father actually dealing with a customer and stared as if frozen. Then they broke into a rapturous welcome. Excusing himself from his customer and instructing one of his staff to "Please come and deal with Mr. Whatever he was called he rushed over to him and embraced him in a bear like hug that threatened to break his ribs, saying "My dear boy. This is wonderful. First we heard that you were missing in action, then that you were found and in Hospital but now you are here. Come let us go to the Talbot Arms for lunch." With that he was whisked out of the shop, his protests that "but I need to order a new uniform" brushed aside with "Yes, but that can wait" Soon he found himself sitting before a large helping of 'Steak and Kidney pie' answering her father's flood of questions about his 'recent adventures' as he insisted in calling them. Finally, when his host's mouth was full of pie and, therefore he remained quiet for a few moments he said "I should tell you. I want to marry your daughter!" A few seconds passed while his prospective father-in-law emptied his mouth. Then he asked" But have you asked her and what did she say?" He replied "She said 'Do I get any say in this matter?' I told her NO" His host laughed, saying "That's my girl. I am delighted but have you considered the religious aspects? As I'm sure you are aware, we are Jewish and......." Before his host could say more he interrupted, saying "I've already sought advice on the matter. Since a child borne of a Jewish mother is, automatically a Jew, this is not a problem. Further, I would be prepared to give you my word that our children will receive instruction in Judaism. That only leaves the wedding which could be a civil one..." At this point her father stopped him. Putting his hand on his arm, laughing quietly he said "Yes my boy, I know all this and you are right but I was thinking about the reaction that your own family may have. We Jews are not always popular and you may encounter resentment from some quarters, even bigotry. There are those who like to quote the old adage:

'It was odd of God
to choose the Jews."

Before her father could continue, he interrupted and added

But not so odd as those who choose
A Jewish God and scorn the Jews.

Her father laughed and slapped his thigh. "Who taught you that?" he asked.

"My Grandmother" he said. 'Well' her father replied 'Your Grandmother was right"

He went on to say "I've already spoken with my immediate family. There will be no problems there. As for the rest, I don't care but I don't want her to be ostracised by her own folk" Her father smiled, saying "I can assure you that this will not happen".

So they returned to the shop in the 'Victoria and Albert Arcade' where he was duly measured for his new uniform, then he took his leave. As he left the shop her father called after him "May I tell Momma your news?" He smiled and asked "Could I stop you?"

Now, feeling as though he floated on air he made his way to Milford Central Post Office where he wrote out a telegram form. Addressed to Her at Etaple. It read:

Get leave. Come home. Marry me"

Handing his message over to a lady counter assistant he asked "Please send this to the address shown. When will she receive it and how much do I owe you?"

The lady read the message and smiled "The young lady will receive this tomorrow morning" she said.

The following afternoon he received her reply. It read;

If your last remark is a proposal, the answer is Yes. Regarding your other remarks, you may recall that there is a war on. Nevertheless, I shall do my best

But the German offensive had been halted and now, under pressure from allied counter attacks where falling back on the Hindenburg line. On September 27th, their much vaunted Siegfried Stellung was breached and the enemy was in retreat. But the allies, particularly the British were suffering sobering casualties and her request for leave was not greeted favourably, something she could not quarrel with.

She wrote to say that she had heard from her parents who told her of his conversation with her father but that they urged that she and he should be patient a little longer. The war was not yet over and that the future was not theirs to see, a point of view that he found his mother agreed with. It was, he thought a diplomatic way of saying that he still may be killed, or worse. This did nothing to cool his or her ardour, in fact if anything it inflamed it but he could see the logic in their argument. He loved her too much to want her to spend the rest of her life nursing a cripple or someone who was no longer sane.

One evening he received a visit from Mr Wilkins his old primary school Headmaster, a man he remembered as a short straight backed disciplinarian but now an old man with a mop of steel grey hair and a kindly expression who, like him walked with the aid of a stick' and told his mother, when she answered his knock at the door that he "had come to see his old pupil who had done well and become a hero!", an introduction that made him cringe. Seated opposite him by the fireplace he asked 'Would he care to address the school about how he had won his Military Medal?' When he told his former Head Master that he had no idea, saying "All I can say is that it came up with the rations" Mr Wilkins smiled at his Mother saying "Such commendable modesty!" He then asked "but perhaps you could tell them, particularly the boys about some of the heroic deeds you have witnessed?" He replied "Many of the things I have seen Headmaster are hardly matters to describe to children. Yes, I have seen people do some pretty selfless things but the word 'Heroics' hardly describes a modern war. I could tell them that, many times I have cowered in absolute terror and prayed 'Please Jesus, make it stop!' but he never did." The old man looked at him, clearly saddened and said "Well, yes. Perhaps you are right my boy".

One afternoon towards the end of his leave he answered a knock on the door to find a Mr.Fields, an elderly neighbour standing before him with tear filled eyes and trembling lip. Holding out a crumpled telegram form he asked "How am I to tell her. What can I say to her? She'd just gone to the shops when this came." The telegram stated that their son, a soldier serving in France had died of wounds. Taking Mr Wainwreight's arm he led him into the house, seated him by the fire and called out "Mum! Make Mr Fields a cup of tea" Then he said "I'll go up to the shops. I'll find her. I'll tell her for you!"

He met Mrs Fields walking back from the local shops, wicker shopping basket on her arm. She smiled when she first saw him, striding up the hill towards her, then her smile faded when it was not returned. Taking her shopping basket from her, he told her the news as gently as he could. She took a small embroidered handkerchief from her pocket and tabbed her eyes. Then she said "I think I have known these last two days".

So soon his leave had ended and he reported to the Regimental Depot situated on the outskirts of market town some ten miles north of York and known as Shiretown .

His first appointment was with a medical board of three Medical Officers who were to consider his standard of physical fitness, Their conclusion was that, as long as he needed the aid of a stick he was not fit enough for active duty. His first response was "then can I be posted to Etaple as an Instructor?" The Board's reply was 'No. The Army has all the instructional staff it needs at Etaple. What the Army did desperately need were experienced platoon leaders such as he, but not platoon leaders who walked with the aid of a stick. Therefore he would undertake an intensive course of physical therapy, the aim of which being to bring him back to an A1 category as soon as possible'. Now he and several others like him were placed in the hands of a Sergeant Physical Training Instructor who first accompanied them on ever longer bicycle rides, riding at the front of their column shouting abusive remarks about the inability of his charges to keep up. Then their bicycles were taken from them and now they went on longer and longer runs down country lanes, pursued by their Sergeant who had not given up his bicycle nor his abusive calls if the pace slackened. But the Sergeant's endeavours paid off. His legs began to strengthen, his limp to disappear.

He hated life at the Depot. It appeared to be staffed by old fogies who seemed to have no idea about what the war in France was really like and who spoke of nothing but 'Company Drill ' and 'March discipline'. Nor did he make himself popular when he clashed with the pay office where he claimed that he was owed a considerable sum of money by way of back pay. He was told that this was not so, that what he saw as a short fall was because British Officers do not receive payment when they were held captive by the enemy. So this period would apply from when he was posted 'missing, believed dead' until the Americans reported that he was in their hands; He pointed out that part of that period he was not in captivity but 'on the run' Their reply was that there was no way they could verify how long this was. His impatient retort that perhaps next time he went on the run, he should ask the German Guards for a signed chit!' This remark earned him a stern scowl.

Does it matter ? - Losing your legs ?
For people will always be kind.

Does it matter ? - Losing your sight ?
There's such wonderful work for the blind

Does it matter? – Those dreams from the pit ?
You can drink and forget and be glad.
And people won't think you are mad:
For they'll know that you've fought for your country
And no one will worry a bit.

From a poem by Siegfried Sassoon

18 And Then it Ended

Men fought like fiends; and hideous things were done
And you have nourished hatred, harsh and blind
But in that Golgotha perhaps you'll find
The mothers of the men who killed your son.

Siegfried Sassoon. 1918

Then came November. and the war seemed to end almost as quickly as it had started. When he heard the news he felt quite empty, a little depressed even, surprisingly resentful. Now there was life without war, how could that be? No more not knowing if you would be alive at the end of the day. The fact that he could expect to die in old age was a prospect he could not quiet grasp. He heard two Regular Army Officers discussing the news. One saying "Thank God that it's over. Now we can get back to real soldiering". He found this remark to be astonishing. "What" he thought "has the last four years been about if it wasn't soldiering?" The following morning a strange quiet seemed to have settled on the Depot. Many did not bother to fall in for morning parade, so the Colonel took the diplomatic course and cancelled it. He heard that someone had tipped the contents of a fire bucket over the head of the Regimental Sergeant Major and that, at 10:00AM the Sergeant of the Guard told his men "I'm going to bugger off for a bit, but I'll expect you to be here when I come back" – which they were. Other than that, by the second day of peace, Depot life seemed to have returned to normal. That second day, whilst taking his evening meal a fellow diner, an officer who, like him was back at the Depot after suffering a wound asked him "Now its over, what do you plan to do?" He had to admit that, at least for the moment he had no idea, adding "After all, I was only sixteen when I enlisted. But what about you. What are your plans?" He was amazed to hear his fellow diner say "Oh. I'll go into politics" "But" he asked him "You can't just 'go into politics'. Surely you must be invited to join a political party?" "No" replied the other "To get into politics join any political party doing anything. That's how one gets into politics and that's how one can make money" His fellow diner had served as the Intelligence Officer with a battalion in

France. Years later, looking back to this conversation he realized that this officer had been well suited for his post for he was indeed, very intelligent. Or was he just very ruthless?

Early in January 1919 she came home, having been released from her duties at the General Hospital at Etaple. Early spring they married at the Registrar's office in Milltown Town Hall. Only a few people from both families attended, her friend, a fellow nurse and his younger sister acting as witnesses.

But her mother or Momma as she preferred to be called was not to be denied a celebration. She and her husband had hired the village hall near their family home and in it had organised a reception or 'After Party' as she preferred to call it. So, after the ceremony that is where they retired to find, awaiting them a considerable crowd of friends and relations, although the later were mainly hers. Here trestle tables, arranged in the form of an inverted U were covered in starched table clothes and decorated with bunches of fresh cut flowers, small printed cards at each place named the occupant. The seating plan ensured that guests from both families were mixed.

A small group of musicians were seated in a corner of the room, awaiting their turn to provide the entertainment.

He and his bride took their seats at the head of the tables, her parents seated on their daughters left, his mother and sisters seated to his right. Their guests taking their seats down the other sides of the arrangement.

First, after ensuring that all guest had been served with a glass of a sweet red wine, her father asked all to raise their glasses and drink a toast to the happy couple, wishing them both health and happiness. Now the musicians began to play and everyone sang;

"Siman Tov Omazal Tov,

Mazal Tov Vewsiman Tov ",

Then applause, laughter and calls wishing the couple everything good in life.

Now everyone was served first with a plate of chopped liver. This was followed by chicken soup and then a main course of chicken served with a choice of either rice or potatoes. Rice in lieu of potatoes was new to him but it was an alternative which he found to be enjoyable. For a dessert they were served a typical Yorkshire dish of 'Bread and Butter Pudding'. His mother whispered to him "Well, this certainly beats ham sandwiches at the Chapel!!!" This caused him to chuckle almost uncontrollably so that, to conceal his mirth he had to place his hand over his mouth. When his bride asked "Is this a private joke or may I share it? All he could say was "I promise to tell you later!

Then more toasts in a drink of each persons choice, some of which his bride whispered was produced at home by her Mother and in large quantities for occasions such as this. Once the meal was over and the tables cleared, the small group of musicians began to play music which were new to him but not to her relatives who raised their voices in songs such as "Amm Israel Hai" and again "Mazal Tov" .Everyone sang in such harmony and with such an outpouring of joy and happiness directed towards himself and his bride that he felt his lip tremble with the emotion of the moment. But now violins were put aside and, taking up saxophone, clarinet and cornet the musicians began to play the latest 'Ragtime' music and people began to dance, but first the Bride and Groom were required to take the floor. His protest that "But I can't dance was brushed aside with "then I'll teach you!" Soon they were making at least a gallant attempt. Two of her uncles, single men probably in their early forties soon insisted that his younger sister and his 'Auntie Nellie', a comely war widow in her late twenties, despite their protests join the dancing. Soon her uncles, both outrageous flirts were teaching them all the modern dance steps. Both ladies were soon in a seventh heaven, particularly his sister who squealed and giggled with sheer delight, skirts twirling around her calves as she was whirled around the floor dancing 'The Lindy Hop' , 'The Turkey Trot' , The Fox Trot, The Cake walk, 'The Black Bottom' and even 'The Tango'.

Then, in the early evening he and his Bride bade their guests' farewell, leaving the 'After Party' still in full swing and departed for the Railway station to take the evening train to the east coast where they were to spend their honeymoon.

They found a compartment all to themselves where they were able to take stock of the fact that, yes now they were a couple. Once the train began to move she asked him what his mother had said that he had found so funny. He repeated the remark which once again gave him a fit of giggles. When she said that she didn't think it was that funny, he replied "Then you should try those Chapel ham sandwiches!" This reduced them both to helpless laughter. When they had both regained their composure she said "Now I must tell you something else which is also better than Chapel ham sandwiches" He asked "What would that be?" She replied "I think I'm pregnant!"

Having been 'one of the first to join' he was released from the Army shortly after he returned to the Depot following his 'Honeymoon' leave'. He did consider taking up Colonel Baxter's offer to support an application for a regular commission but decided that the army life and family life would not necessarily be compatible. So he came home, a young man of twenty one who, like those men he first went into the line with knew things about life beyond his years. Now he had to make a new life which would include his woman and their child. A daunting responsibility.

Above her fathers shop in the Victoria and Albert Arcade was a suite of rooms, really intended to be 'stock rooms' but which consisted of two rooms, a kitchenette and a combined toilet and bathroom. Her father agreed that they could convert these into their first abode. So, there followed a week of scrubbing and cleaning, then painting and papering to change it to their liking. Then, using the small gratuity he had been paid by the Army, - £150 to be paid in four instalments plus 52 shillings for a civilian suit of clothes -, she marched him to every second hand furniture shop in the town. An old thread bare 'three piece suite' was bought for a song and immediately placed in the hands of an 'Upholsterer' who was to ' reupholster in a material of her choosing, the material being, of course a 'bit left over from a bigger job;.. A similar purchase was a scratched and battered dinning table and four chairs which were despatched to a 'French Polisher'. Her mother ran up soft furnishing such as cushion covers, curtains etc. on her treadle powered Singer sewing machine, which she considered to be a product of white hot technology. The material she used was purchased from an establishment which she referred to as 'the Fent Shop!'

An old iron bedstead was ruthlessly scrubbed to bare metal with a wire brush then repainted and fitted with a new mattress. Two old carpets were taken to her parents' house, hung over a line in the back garden and beaten and beaten until his wrists screamed in agony and he thought he would choke in the resulting clouds of dust. For bedding, table ware, cutlery, crockery etc., their wedding presents provided most of their needs. So they had a nest. Now to find a way to make a living. Her father offered him a position in his shop, performing some function which he knew was in invention so he thanked him and turned the offer down.

His first endeavours in the labour market were not encouraging, one particularly so. A rather plump and balding man who interviewed him hooked his thumbs into his waistcoat so as to expose his gold watch chain and asked "Well. What were you?" A bit puzzled by the question, he said to the balding man "I'm sorry but I don't understand what you mean" The balding man then said in a sarcastic tone "Well, what did you do?" He replied "I became an infantry Officer. A Lieutenant. A platoon commander" The balding man said "Well, there isn't much call for Platoon Commanders now" then added "Sorry, but your too old to be taught owt" (Owt , a Yorkshire expression meaning 'anything'). As he left the balding man called after him "The Nation will never forget you!" Feeling pretty crestfallen he walked back to where he had left her, sitting on a park bench doing the crossword in the morning paper. Seeing him approach she got up and ran to meet him, asking "How did you get on?" He replied "He told me I was 'too old to be taught OWT'', then as I was leaving he called after me 'The Nation will never forget you'" Smiling up into his gloomy face she tucked her hand into his arm and said "What a silly man. You are the Nation!" Then she added, "Never mind him dear, we'll manage"

The next morning, as they ate breakfast she suddenly reached for a pencil and drew a circle around something she saw in the Yorkshire Post she was reading and passed the paper over to him' The item she had circled was in the 'Public Notices' column. It said that the Board of Education was to sponsor courses of two years duration to train those who wished to become teachers. The salary would be £102 per annum. He looked up to find her watching him intently across the table. She said "We still have most of your gratuity, I have a few savings and we can live here 'rent free'. We could manage until you are qualified"

So he applied. And that is what he did.

The Train

A train was pulling into the platform but it was pulled by a steam engine. It pulled a long line of old style carriages, but in immaculate condition. "Where on earth would you find such examples?" he thought. He hadn't seen anything like these since the 1950's. The Station Master was standing on the platform shouting 'Express Service only.' 'Express Service only.' She was there, leaning out of a carriage window, waving to him. She seemed to be wearing that navy blue jacket and that damned hat; surely she hadn't kept it all these years. She looked so young, like she looked that day at the fishing quay. A broad smile spread across his face and he sprinted down the platform towards her. Amazing, he thought, he didn't know he could still sprint.

He was still smiling when they found him the following morning, sitting outside his shed at the allotment. The blackbird had returned to his perch, still singing his serenade.

The Minstrel boy will return we pray
Torn in body, perhaps but not in spirit

**Patriotism is not enough.
I must bear hatred for no man.**

Nurse Edith Cavell, Brussels 1915

www.ingramcontent.com/pod-product-compliance
Lightning Source LLC
Chambersburg PA
CBHW041407010726
47507CB00001B/23

9780992846503